A NO EXCEPTIONS NOVEL

the

Lover's Promise

J.C. REED

Cover art by Larissa Klein

Editing by Shannon Wolfman & Katherine Tomlinson

ISBN: 1507596308
ISBN-13: 978-1507596302

If you don't fight for what you love and yearn,

Don't mourn what could have been.

In life there are rules; in love no exceptions.

- J.C. Reed

Chapter 1

JETT

New York City, 3 days earlier.

THE PAST WAS the past, and the future would be nothing but whatever I made of it. My future was her, our lives interlinked with our hopes and our dreams, and long-forgotten plans. Strange to think that only a few months ago I never thought my life or I would change. I never thought that an encounter with a future employee would result in me actually wanting to take the next step and marry her.

Sitting in the bar, my heart sped up at the thought of

3

what still lay ahead of me. The initial plans had been set in motion. Now it was time to execute them. I was going to do whatever it'd take to distract her, and then in exactly four hours and twenty-five minutes I'd propose to her, after which I'd whisk her away in a private plane for a quick surprise wedding in Las Vegas, leaving my friends to finish the rest of my arrangements and carry out my revenge.

It was supposed to be a simple plan, one I had organized for a long time. Now if only she would say "yes" and play along.

Granted, a marriage proposal came a bit soon in our relationship, maybe too soon, but I had no option—not if my plan was going to work. Soon, he'd find out I'd betrayed him, and he'd try to hurt her to get back at me. The thought of losing her to someone else, of my enemies finding her, made me crazy with rage. For her, to save her from the ones who wanted to hurt her and were after her, I would kill.

Marrying was the least of my problems, not least because I knew deep down that I was ready. Call me foolish, call me desperate. Fuck, call me vengeful, but in my heart I knew what I was doing was the right thing—for her, for us. And while I did not want to control her, I had every intention of doing whatever it might take to make her mine by law. And if by any chance, she wouldn't accept my proposal, or if she needed more time because I was moving too fast for her, then I'd bend her to my will until she realized we belonged together.

"So, this is your big night, huh?" Tiffany's voice penetrated the dark haze covering my mind, drawing my attention back to her. Looking up at one of my oldest friends, I frowned and swallowed down a snarky remark. I hated disruptions, and in particular the kind that took me by surprise when I was immersed in my thoughts. But Tiffany had always had my back, and right now, I couldn't afford to piss her off—not when she was helping me out with my somewhat illegal scheme.

"You could say that." My gaze met her sharp, blue eyes. "Did you get it?"

Tiffany nodded her head. "Custom-made, specifically designed for her." She put a black gift bag on the table and pushed it toward me. "Just as you asked."

My heart fluttered as I pulled a little velvet box out of the bag, my fingers hovering over the soft fabric. For a short moment fear choked me and dark thoughts gathered at the back of my mind. This better not be a mistake. It better be perfect. Of course there was a chance that I might be ruining everything, but as decisions went, I hardly ever backed down on them, so I pushed my dark thoughts away and opened the black case. Relief streamed in waves through me when my eyes caught the ring.

It was a delicate assemblage of gemstones with a two-carat diamond in the middle. Sparkling and gleaming in the soft light of the club, much like Brooke's eyes, which were the reason I had fallen in love with her, it was more beautiful than I had ever envisioned.

The tiny engraving read:

With no exceptions, my love for you doesn't need reciprocation to exist.

Jett x

The setting felt delicate and my decision final. I turned it around a few times, wondering how a piece of metal could feel both delicate and grave at the same time. Now my plans felt more real than ever. Brooke would like it, no doubt about that, but would she say "yes?" As if sensing my doubts, Tiffany cleared her throat, her soft voice drawing my attention back to the conversation at hand.

"She'll love it, Jett. I know it," she whispered, her eyes on the ring.

I suppressed a smile. "Brooke's like no other woman I've ever met. For all I know, she might just throw it at my head when she finds out what I'm really up to."

She let out a laugh. "You're right, I don't know her. But I know she'd be crazy not to like it, especially after you went all the trouble to get it perfect." She pointed at the ring. My gaze moved from her to our laser-inscribed names. They looked alien like they didn't belong to us, and for a moment it all seemed like a strange dream, the past few months eerily surreal. Was that what love was all about? Experiencing a string of events that would all slip away and mold into bittersweet memories?

Forcing my eyes away from the ring, I put it back it into the box and dropped the box back into the gift bag. "Thanks for doing it at such a short notice, Ti. I knew I could count on you to get it done within twenty-four hours."

She flicked her hand. "Don't mention it. Being friends with the owner of the shop has its perks." She smiled softly and leaned forward. "Whatever you need, just call me and it's a done deal." For a short moment, silence ensued between us during which she stirred her coffee with a teaspoon. "So, when does it start?"

"Tonight at dinner. Everything's finished." I returned her smile in a weak moment of excitement rushing through me.

"Have you told her about Nate yet?"

My smile died like a blown-out candle. "About my brother being let out of prison today?" I raised my eyebrows and snorted. "You're kidding, right?"

"What about you visiting with him the past few weeks? Another secret you'll be taking to the grave?"

"Now's not the time." I shook my head, more at myself than at Tiffany. Would there ever be a right moment?

"Seriously?" She stared at me for a few seconds, her face suddenly devoid of any emotion, and then her lips parted slowly, as though she wanted to say something but couldn't bring herself to. I set my jaw. Of course she didn't understand; I didn't expect she would. "You should tell her, dude," Tiffany finally said. "Trust me, if she knew you kept secret like that, you'd be in big trouble. This whole scheme of yours will blow right in your face if you don't tell her."

"No, Ti. Not happening," I said with as much conviction as I could. "Brooke can't know about it."

"All right," she whispered under her breath and took a sip of her coffee. Running her hand through her black hair, she leaned back, regarding me with curiosity. "You sure this is what you want, Jett?" She inclined her head toward the black gift bag, a strange smile playing on her lips. I knew she was referring to the marriage part because she had tried to broach the subject a few times—without much success.

"I'm sure. I've been waiting for this day for a while now and to be honest, I wouldn't know a better time."

"Because she doesn't suspect." It was more a statement than a question.

"Yes," I said slowly, ignoring the way her eyes seemed to pierce through me, as if there was something she knew and I didn't. Watching her, I was reminded once more that there was something different about her. Not the hair she wore dyed black now, nor the weight she had lost; her

8

entire demeanor had changed. Ever since I had returned to the gang, she seemed different, almost unrecognizable. The past years had been hard on her; her alcohol addiction had turned her into a shell of her former radiant self; her once carefree attitude replaced with weariness and aloofness.

"Do you remember last year?" The question came suddenly, taking me by surprise.

I frowned at her, unsure where she was heading.

Last year? I hadn't known Brooke back then. As much as my first impulse demanded that I ask what the fuck she was talking about, I didn't. I sensed she was treading onto personal terrain that had nothing to do with my brother, Nate, nor with Brooke and my decision to marry her.

It was only when Tiffany leaned forward, cocking her head to the side with a soft smile on her lips, that it dawned on me.

"You and me?" she prompted. "Don't even tell me you never miss it, Jett."

I stared at her, then cringed inwardly. Tiffany was talking about our past. Not any past, but ours. The one before Brooke and lots of other women. Faces I couldn't remember, let alone put a name to them. A part of me wanted to stop Tiffany's words from flowing, but it was too late.

"I know you better than anyone out there, Jett," she whispered and touched my arm gently. "Look at me and tell me in all honesty. Can you really say to my face that you don't miss it?"

Fuck!

It was a question I had dreaded for years. A question that still made me feel uncomfortable to the point of wanting to leave and never look back. A question I thought she'd never dare ask because, surely, deep inside she knew the truth. I hadn't expected it now, hours before I'd get down on one knee in front of another woman and ask her to build with me the kind of family I never had. Tiffany and I hadn't talked about the past in a long time, and that was just the way I liked it. Everything before Brooke wasn't worth mentioning or remembering. In retrospect, I realized I should never have asked Tiffany to meet with me. It had been a stupid move. But Tiffany and I had been friends so long, that I thought she had moved on a long time ago.

Catching the way she was looking at me with a glimmer of hope in her eyes, a look I had seen so many times after meaningless dates, something else dawned on me. Tiffany might be one of my oldest friends and dating Brian, but as a woman she was like each and every one of my past lovers: weak. She wasn't over our breakup. Fuck, she might even be in love with me, and there wasn't shit I could do about it.

"All the things we did? All the fun we had?" she prompted when I remained silent.

"It's over, Ti. You know that," I said as softly as I could, ignoring the touch of her fingertips on my arm.

She shook her head, and the smile on her lips widened.

"You said the exact same thing last time, but you forget that I know you, Jett. *The real you.*" She moved closer to me, until I could smell the scent of her perfume, sweet and dark—just like she was. "You aren't the kind of man who's happy with just one woman in his life. You admitted that when you left me after two years. You said success and winning mean everything to you, that you always want more."

The lump in my throat thickened. I swallowed hard, almost choking on it.

She was right, of course. Those were my exact words. I used to be the kind of man who was never happy with just one woman. Fuck, I was the motherfucking asshole who shied away from any sort of commitment that went beyond settling a time for a next date that would end in bed. But worse than that, I left her with no apology, no explanation, and I never broke it off—not officially anyway—because there was nothing to be broken off in the first place.

The truth was we, Tiffany and I, had never been exclusive. I had always assumed she understood what that meant. After all, we had agreed to date whomever who wanted. And we had. Or maybe, to be more precisely, my dick had. One woman a night. Not one single second chance. Not a single second date. I had so many I lost count. There was no doubt ours had been an open relationship, a friendship with benefits. Tiffany had seen many of those women come and go.

"Last year was a mistake. It was my birthday, and I was drunk," I muttered under my breath.

Actually, Tiffany had gotten me drunk. The way I remembered it, she stayed at my place, reaching for bottle after bottle, insisting that I drank for the both of us.

"What about the other times?" she whispered. "The times before that? Were those a mistake, too?"

I had no answer, and she nodded as if that confirmed her suspicion.

"I miss the times when we were young," Tiffany continued, her voice gaining in confidence and more emotion than I cared for. "We were so in love. We had that amazing chemistry. I know we haven't talked about this in a long time, but…" She paused and brushed her fingers to remove the moisture trailing down her cheek. "Sometimes I wonder what would have happened if I had kept the baby; if things might have taken a different turn."

I clenched my fist under the table. Brooke and I were expecting our first child. Of course it would remind Tiffany of her own child. Her pain was etched in her eyes, but as much as I wanted to say something to take it all away, I couldn't find the right words. I had never been good in

12

dealing with women's emotions.

Fuck, I didn't think I was ever any good in dealing with any of my exes. Even my buddies joked that the way I usually dumped them would scar them for life and spoil their trust in the male population forever.

"Ti." I took a deep breath, ready to say anything to stop her from talking, but the words didn't come out. Even looking at her, feeling the guilt, was hard. I took another deep breath, but the words remained lodged in my throat.

What was I supposed to say to someone who had encountered her fair share of suffering? Someone who had confided in me like I had done so many times in her? Someone who thought I reciprocated her feelings when that couldn't be further from the truth?

"Our room is ready for us. It's the same we used last time." She was standing in front of me now, and the traces of pain in her eyes were replaced by something else, something I feared even more than her reminiscing about the past. It was the look of renewed hope, the kind of look that past lovers have in their eyes when they show up at one's doorstep, hoping for more to the point of being desperate.

"There's always a new beginning, Jett," she continued in a more hopeful tone, oblivious to my thoughts, absorbed in her own world. "You wanted to see me, and that's all that matters. Deep down, I knew we were never over. That you'd come back to me someday."

Her fingers wrapped behind my neck, forcing me to look up, her sinfully red lips coming so close I was instantly reminded of the countless times she had taken me between them, offering me the kind of pleasure that made me forget the shitty world around me. Passion—all raw and gritty and fulfilling—but without the feelings Brooke had stirred inside me. Tiffany leaned forward, whispering in my ear, "I know you think you have to marry her, but really, there are other options, Jett."

I pressed my lips into a tight line.

There was no doubt that Tiffany had seen our sexual relationship as special, but to admit the truth, which was that I never really cared for her more than as a friend would be too hard a blow. I couldn't hurt her more than I had already, but I had to. If only it were easy. If only she and Brian weren't two of my best friends, and the only family I'd ever known It would have been so much easier if she were a mere acquaintance, a random stranger I could walk away from.

Seeing her feelings reflected in her blue eyes, I had no idea how to start. I inhaled a sharp breath and let it out slowly as I made up my mind. Things—no matter how painful—had to be said.

Her kiss came suddenly, catching me off-guard. Her tongue slid into my mouth, eager and hungry. For a second,

I was too stunned to act, overwhelmed by memories of old times intermingled with the distant ringing bell and a faint awareness that Tiffany was in a relationship with the one guy whose trust I couldn't betray.

Something stirred inside me, but it wasn't pleasure. It was pity.

Pity that I didn't feel the same for her as she did for me.

Pity that I didn't want her anymore.

Pity that whatever had happened in the past was long over, that I had moved on from my old me. We had both evolved—in different directions at different speeds.

I grabbed her shoulder and pushed her away more roughly than I intended.

"Ti." I breathed out, struggling for words. "What the fuck!"

I wiped my mouth with the back of my hand, as if the motion could remove the marks of her lipstick and the taste of her lips. As if I could undo my mistakes. It did nothing to lessen the feeling of disgust at her behavior. "What the fuck were you thinking?"

She shrugged. "I thought you wanted to. That's why I booked the room."

"Are you drunk right now? Because if you aren't, I swear I've no idea what's gotten into your fucking head." I regarded her intently, unsure whether to laugh or shake some sense into her.

"What's wrong with you? I've been sober for the past seven years, and I'm very proud of it."

I shook my head. "No, Ti. What's wrong with *you*? You're in a fucking relationship and so am I."

"If it's about Brian, I can explain," Tiffany said softly. "I never thought you'd return to the gang. I never thought I might still feel the same way about you. When you told me you needed me, I knew it was your way of saying that you needed to see me the way you used to in the past."

I stared at her. This was even worse than I had imagined. The whole situation was awkward and I didn't do awkward.

On the one hand, I could understand her confusion. People don't remain friends for no reason. They always fall back into benefits territory, which I had done too many times in the past before I met Brooke. Like last year, when in a desperate mood for sex, she just happened to be available and we hooked up. Time after time. On the other hand, Tiffany always changed when she started drinking. She became unpredictable, difficult to communicate with.

"We shouldn't talk for a while," I said weakly. "Meeting you here was a mistake."

"What are you saying? That this is the wrong place?" She slowly scanned left and right, as if Brian might be lurking around the corner. I snorted inwardly because I doubted he'd just be standing around, watching, if he caught his girlfriend cheating.

"It's not about Brian." I swallowed. "I like you, Ti. I really do, but…"

There was a long pause.

"But what?" she prompted.

"You're like a sister to me."

"A sister?" She stared at me. "No one fucks his sister, Jett."

"You know that's not what I meant." I sighed and ran my hand through my hair. "That will never happen again." My voice betrayed my anger. "What happened between us is over. Do you understand? Nothing will *ever* happen again."

Now it was her turn to look at me, confused and vengeful. I could see her mind trying to glue my words together in order to make sense of them while her heart was slowly breaking.

"It's her, isn't it?" The tone was accusing. "She's younger, and she's pregnant. It's her you want at the moment, but no woman ever lasts with you. They never did in the past and they won't in the future."

"This is different." I turned away. "You knew she's the woman I want to spend the rest of my life with. Those were my exact words when I ordered the ring."

"And yet I thought it was all part of some grand plan of yours." She laughed and brushed her hair out of her eyes.

"You can't blame me because you tend to have quite a few of those."

Fuck, Tiffany had always been good at ignoring the obvious.

"It is, but not the way you might imagine." I wet my lips, unsure whether to elaborate. As much as I trusted Tiffany, I didn't trust her *that* much. "I'm doing it for real, because I want to be with her, not because I'm being forced nor because she's pregnant. If her circumstances didn't demand that I marry her, I'd still be thinking about it. I don't expect you to understand, Ti." I stared her down, my gaze hard. Maybe I hadn't been clear enough. Maybe I needed to be a jerk for her to finally get the hint and move on. "I'm a changed man. What we had was not the same as what I have now with Brooke. So don't tell me who I am. You don't know me anymore. You don't know fuck about me, Ti." As soon as the words came out, hard and accusing, I regretted them. Being a jerk was one thing; being an asshole another.

"I'm sorry." My hands reached out, but it was too late. She flinched as she looked at me as if I had just hit her with a fire lash.

"For what? For telling me the truth? Or for not feeling the same way I do?" She smiled bitterly. "It's not your fault that the truth sucks, Jett."

"I still had no right to be so rude."

"You had *every* right." She looked away, past my shoulders, and took a deep breath. "You might be an asshole for hurting me when you left and then again the day you returned, but it's not your fault for feeling the way you do. I mean..." She sighed. "I knew someday casual sex would no longer be enough for you; I knew you'd find someone who'd make you want to commit. I just hoped I'd never get to see it. I just hoped..."

I hoped it would be me.

The unspoken words lingered in the air.

"Anyway, I'm better off now." Signaling that she was ready to leave, she gathered her coat and bag, barely looking at me. "I'm sorry I won't be at your engagement party, Jett. I have so much stuff to do at work, but I'll make sure to send you a gift."

"Don't do that, Ti."

She held up her hand, stopping me in mid-sentence. "No, it's okay, I want to. I should never have booked that room, anyway. Brian has been good to me; way better than you ever have." Even though her smile indicated that it was all a joke, I didn't miss the sting in her tone. "He didn't deserve all that shit, you know?" She looked up at me. "Please do pass on my best regards to Brooke and tell her...tell her I'm sorry for everything."

I nodded, watching her get up and slide into her coat.

"Will you be okay?" I asked. Opposite from us, a neon

light flickered across the bar area, illuminating countless bottles of alcohol, making them even harder to miss—or resist.

She rolled her eyes and a soft smile lit up her face.

"Look, Jett, I'm fine. And I'm clean. If you think I'm back to my old days of guzzling down booze, you're wrong. So very wrong." She laughed. "I have absolutely no desire for a single drop. The fact that you see me walking into a bar to meet you over a glass of water should be proof enough that I'm long over my addiction." At my skeptical expression her smile widened. "Really, you're making such a fuss. It's like you don't know me at all."

The lie sounded plausible enough—if only I could believe it. If only I hadn't caught the way Tiffany looked at the guy holding his drink. If only she hadn't been so quick to kiss me and act the way she only did when she was drunk. If she cracked, there would never be enough alcohol to sate her addiction and it'd all be my fault.

"Ti…" I began, gathering my words.

"Goodbye, Jett." She flashed me another smile and snatched the bag out of my hand, then leaned forward to plant a kiss on my cheek. "Be good to Brooke. I know you'll make a great husband…and dad." Her eyes lingered on me for a few moments. And then she walked off without waiting for my reply.

Chapter 2

BROOKE

New York City, Present Day

CALM DOWN.
Calm the fuck down.

There was nothing to fear, because I had done nothing wrong. It had been Gina's idea to visit the club, not mine. All I had to do was answer the detective's questions and then I was free to leave.

Countless thoughts raced through my head but only one registered: Gina was dead. Killed. Who would have done it?

And for a handbag? Even as I asked myself those questions, I knew a mugging wasn't the answer. While people stole handbags, they didn't necessarily cut the victim's throat in the process, which was why the detective was here—to unravel the mystery and get to the bottom of things. Like me, he probably suspected foul play and while I hoped he'd find the killer, I also hoped that, just because Thalia and I happened to be the last people who saw Gina alive, we wouldn't end up as persons of interest.

"Jenna?" Grayson's voice drew me back to reality. "You're the first. The detective would like to ask you a few questions now."

Oh, shit.

The icy knot in my stomach intensified, growing as big as an iceberg under the water's surface. Why did I have to go first when I didn't want to? He'd only pour all his energy into grilling me, and I had no answers, no clues, nothing to help out in any way.

Basically, I was doomed to look like I was guilty.

"Great. I'll be happy to help," I said weakly and shot Grayson a confident smile, avoiding the detective's intense stare. To be honest, I had no idea if he remembered our brief encounters at the hotel, but I could feel his gaze burning a hole in my head. When I finally dared look up, I realized his eyes not only rested on me, but there was also a flicker of recognition clearly written on his face. I froze in

22

horror.

This is what happens when you stare at a guy you don't know, Stewart. You come across as a complete creep.

Back then, I had probably looked like a guilty mess to him. I swallowed down the lump in my throat, and tried to behave as innocently as possible.

"Detective, you're welcome to use my office," Grayson said, oblivious to my frayed nerves.

"Thank you. It won't take long," the man said while his stare remained glued to me.

Please, don't leave me alone with him.

I felt like a lamb scheduled to be slaughtered. My skin began to itch from the strain of trying to act casual. I had done nothing wrong, and yet his intense glance made me feel guilty. Talk about unfair. Talk about the crappiest day of my life. The crappiest of all crappy days.

The detective turned on his heels and motioned for me to follow him, and so I did, unsure what would happen next. To the daunting sound of impending doom, we walked into Grayson's office. I was like that woman in white, ready to be sacrificed to King Kong and could almost hear the proverbial drums beating in the background. I felt completely paralyzed with fear. With my heart pounding hard against my chest, I took a seat and waited for the detective to do the same.

He didn't sit down, which was probably a ruse to infuse

respect into a suspect. He wasn't even *that* tall, so under normal circumstances he wouldn't have intimidated me. But there was nothing normal about today.

I peered around me, considering getting out of Grayson's office by faking fainting. I had always wanted to do that, and figured that was the perfect moment, if only to avoid the probing questions and mistrust that would follow. I took a deep breath and let it out slowly, then closed my eyes for a moment, envisioning the scene. Just too bad I wasn't cut out for acting. In my head, I promised myself that I'd sign up for some much-needed acting classes. That is, if I ever made it out of here and saved up enough money.

The detective turned the knob and closed the door behind him.

Now we were alone.

Just he and I—behind a closed door.

Dum. Dum Dum.

No, make that *doom*. Doom—as the imaginary drums continued to pound in my head.

My whole body began to shake slightly as he slid into Grayson's seat and pulled out a notepad from his pocket. The whole situation felt surreal, like I was starring in a horror movie. I almost expected him to retrieve a string of rope and tie up my wrists to the chair, maybe even switch on a neon lamp, or hang me upside down to torture me into giving him the answers he wanted.

Only, I had no answers.

Let the witch hunt begin.

Sighing, I crossed my arms over my chest, ready to face whatever the detective would throw at me.

He glanced around the room and his eyes came to rest on the model pictures on the wall. Grayson's glory. The gems he'd shaped into diamonds—as he liked to proclaim. Every one of his models was up there; everyone but me. It wasn't that much of a surprise, given that I was new and had yet to book a job. A short silence ensued, during which Detective Barrow assessed me, his right hand stroking his neck in a strange manner. I twitched uncomfortably in my chair and crossed my legs, waiting, assessing him back.

"So, Mr. Grayson told me you joined two days ago. Is that correct?" he started eventually.

"Yes." I nodded, staring at him blankly and gradually relaxed, happy that he didn't ask about the hotel. Maybe he didn't remember me after all. Maybe it was just a normal investigation and his frown came as a part of the job description, meaning it had nothing to do with me personally.

"All right." He smiled politely and opened his notepad. "Let's start with the last time you saw Gina alive and we'll take it from there. You mentioned you went out?"

It wasn't a question, but rather a statement. I had

mentioned no such thing to him.

I nodded. "After Grayson offered me a trial period to see whether I was cut out for the job, Thalia invited me and Gina for a drink at the La Rue Bar. We had a few drinks, then Gina suggested we visit the Hush Hush bar, and we had some more drinks there."

God, why did it sound like I was a complete party girl when it couldn't be further from the truth?

The detective nodded and scribbled a few words on his notepad without looking up. "What happened after?"

"Gina tried to hook me up with a guy." *Cringe.* I didn't need to hear the detective's thoughts; I could *read* them from his expression and they weren't pretty. I brushed my hair out of my face and continued. "I started to feel sick so a guy brought me home. And that was the last time I saw her."

I repeated the same story I had told Thalia: that a stranger drove me home, and then left. "Thalia said she had one last drink with Gina after I left. What happened after that, I don't know. You'll have to ask her."

"The man who drove you home—" He stopped scribbling and looked up from his pad, his eyes the color of brown parchment assessing me. "—what did you say his name was?"

"I don't remember," I lied. "I was too drunk."

The detective pressed his lips in a tight line. The way he

was drumming his fingers on the table made me nervous, so I looked away, mentally counting the seconds until I could get the hell out.

"Did anything strange happen yesterday? Such as a fight, not necessarily between you and the victim?" I shook my head and he continued, "Can you think of anyone who might have held a grudge against her?"

A new spasm of nerves coursed through me.

"No, of course not." I brushed my hair out of my face as I considered my words carefully. "I only just met her so didn't know her particularly well, but it seemed Gina is…was friendly with all the girls here. I think everyone liked her."

"How was the relationship between Gina and Thalia?"

I paused, taken aback by the strange question. "Good, I guess. I think they were good friends. Like I said, I only met them both recently."

"If anything unusual happened, no matter how trivial you think it might be, I need you to tell me. It's the little things that often carry enough weight to break a case. Do you understand?" He stared at me. "They're often relevant."

His tone worried me.

"I wish I could be of more help, but I don't remember much, except that Gina brought us drinks," I said carefully. "We got drunk. We had fun. And the next thing I knew a guy drove me home."

Even though I omitted quite a bit, I stuck to the truth. My mind had been a blurry mess. Yesterday's events seemed so far away, they almost resembled a dream. The only thing I remembered was the way Jett had broken my fall, and the fake name he had given me, but I couldn't share that with the detective. For some inexplicable reason, I couldn't tell anyone about the Jett incident. It was like my brain wanted to lock that episode away forever.

When I finally finished my account, the detective opened a folder on the table. "Maybe these pictures will jolt your memory." Slowly, he began to sort through countless sheets of paper and pictures.

"Did Gina wear this makeup when you last saw her?" He slid over the first picture and I shrank back in shock.

It was a headshot of Gina. For a second, it looked like she was sleeping, until I registered that her eyes were slightly open, and a dried trail of blood marked her chin. There was no doubt the picture had been taken after her death and the discovery of her body. The rest of her body from the neck down wasn't in the picture. If there were, I knew I would have needed therapy for the next few years.

"What do you mean?" I asked slowly. Her face and lips were so pale they almost had a blue shimmer to them. I had never seen a corpse in real life, not even when my father and my sister died.

The detective pointed his finger to her left cheek. "Did she have the two spots on her face?"

I narrowed my eyes in concentration and finally grasped the meaning of his words. There were two dots on her cheek—like two little moles or freckles. Come to think of it, they didn't really stand out. They had been painted onto the skin in a fashionable but realistic way so that it wasn't glaringly obvious that they weren't real.

"No, " I said and shook my head. "Not as far as I remember."

He nodded, as if my answer confirmed his suspicion, and handed me the second picture.

"Do you recognize this man?" he asked.

I looked from the detective to the picture, and my heart froze.

Holy mother of grace.

That couldn't possibly be. I blinked several times as an array of emotions washed over me.

Staring back at me was Jett's face.

But how?

I was so shocked, I couldn't utter a word. Under the desk, I balled my hands into fists to stop myself from reacting. From screaming. From showing the waves of panic shooting through me.

Why was he showing me a picture of Jett?

It didn't make any sense. I scanned the picture once

more in the hope that it might be someone else. But it was really Jett. His handsome face. Sitting in a chair, with a whiskey glass in his hand, his mind lost in thought and a million miles away, just like I had found him the previous night at the bar. The image seemed to have been taken from a security camera inside the club.

"This photo was taken yesterday," the detective explained. "It's the second time a woman was killed after leaving the club. The first murder took place two weeks ago. Both women had the same two moles painted on their faces. The first victim had one, the second two." He tapped his finger against Jett's blurry shape. "I'm aware this is a bad photograph, and I apologize for that. Maybe this one might help jog your memory."

From the folder he retrieved a third picture and slid it across the table. "Have a look. This was taken on the same day, two hours before the first victim was killed. Someone sent it to us, and while we don't have concrete evidence yet, it still connects our suspect to the first victim."

I swallowed hard, unable to breathe. What was he saying? What did he mean by "suspect" and "connects to the victim"?

Blood began to rush in my ears as I regarded the photograph on the table. Compared to the previous ones, it looked like a professional shot—large in size and with excellent pixilation—the kind a private detective would make. I wrought my hands together, ignoring the pang of pain as my nails pierced the thin barrier of my skin, and forced myself to take in all the details. Jett was wearing his usual expensive suit and carrying two cups of what I assumed was coffee. A young woman was standing next to him and, judging from her slightly open mouth and the fact that she was turned to him, it looked as though she was talking to him. I had no idea who she was, but there were other people around them and from the ambience I recognized one of the coffee shops not far from our office building. There was no time stamp on the photo; nothing to give away what was going on, except that Jett had been buying coffee for two. He didn't seem particularly engrossed in whatever the woman was saying, but the way her body was turned to him—a little too close—while she looked up straight at him made me wonder why he seemed so lost in thought, almost as if he was considering what to say in reply to her.

"So, do you recognize him?" the detective asked, disrupting my trail of thought. "He's our primary suspect."

As slowly as I could, I forced myself to shake my head. Even if I wanted to, I couldn't talk. I was too shocked. Too afraid that any word I might utter would betray the truth. Too afraid that the truth would shatter me. Too afraid of everything—and in particular of not knowing what the hell was going on.

"Who did you say this was again?" I asked in a hushed tone, faking innocence as best as I could, but beneath the layers of nonchalance, my voice was shaking. I prayed silently that if the detective sensed it, he'd assume it was because I was afraid of the killer. Just to be sure, I added nervously, "I can't believe she's dead."

"The victim's name is Sarah Smith. The man in the picture is Jett Mayfield."

Upon hearing Jett's name, I bit my tongue hard to suppress a sharp intake of air.

The detective regarded me for a moment before he continued, "We've been watching him for some time, ever since we received this picture. Earlier today we found his car abandoned two miles from the club. The tires had traces of Gina's DNA on them, which links him to the murder scene."

I didn't know much about evidence, but even to me that sounded incriminating enough. Alarm bells began to ring somewhere in my head.

Jett wasn't a killer. I opened my mouth and closed it an instant later because I couldn't tell the detective the truth. I couldn't reveal that I knew Jett, that we had once dated, that he was the father of my unborn child.

I knew Jett. Maybe not as well as I once thought, but good enough to be convinced that he wasn't a killer. His brother was.

32

But the truth was I didn't know for sure.

Jett had never been an open book. He liked to keep secrets. He had sides to him I didn't know about; sides I was afraid to learn of. He had accompanied me home, but I couldn't say for sure he had stayed with me throughout the entire night.

"You said you found traces on the car," I began warily. "But I thought Gina was stabbed in the street." I kept my voice deliberately low, so he wouldn't hear the turmoil in my tone. As I stared at Jett's face in utter dismay, my heart continued to hammer in my chest. For a few moments, I was afraid to look up out of fear the detective would see right through me.

"She was. Someone ran her over with a car after her throat was cut open. This is all we know for now until we get the autopsy report next week," the detective said.

I felt sick to the core, I feared I might just vomit. My legs were shaking so bad, I knew if I if I weren't sitting down, my legs would have given way under me.

"I'm sorry about your friend," the detective said, misinterpreting my silence. "We're doing the best we can to find out what happened."

"Did you arrest this man?" I asked quietly. Every fiber of my being screamed.

"No. We had to let him go." The detective sounded pissed off. "Unless we have undeniable, concrete proof we have to treat him as not guilty. People with money always get preferential treatment." He grimaced and spat out the word "money" as though it was pure evil, then handed me his card. "If you see him or remember anything, no matter how trivial, call me. We need all the evidence we can get. It's in everyone's best interest to keep the city safe from people like him."

I nodded. He smiled gently, and as I stood, I forced myself to return his smile. On shaky feet, I gathered all the courage I could muster and left Grayson's office, heading straight for the bathroom.

As I splashed my face with cold water, the numbness resulting from shock began to wear off and complete realization kicked in.

The police thought Jett was a killer.

And I had just lied to them. I didn't even know why I didn't just reveal that I knew him. Why was I protecting him? Maybe because I couldn't believe Jett was a killer.

But what if he was?

What if he was…the thought was too horrible, too depressing, too shocking to continue. It broke my heart to think that the man I loved could be capable of killing innocents, so I decided to push it to the back of my mind instead of dealing with the consequent implications.

Chapter 3

MY MIND REELED as I said goodbye to Grayson, then called a taxi and gave the driver Sylvie's address. Snuggled in the backseat, I rested my head against the window, the coldness intensifying the icy shudders that had been circling through my body ever since I saw Jett's face on the snapshot inside the detective's folder.

I felt physically sick. From all the possible things in life, this was what I had expected the least. It had to be a mistake—a stupid, silly mistake—because Jett was a lot of things, but most certainly not a killer. But what if I was blindly in love and not seeing him for who he truly was?

As much as I had hoped the detective had confused him with his brother, I knew it was impossible. Even though

Nate was not his biological brother, the two of them looked alike. But Nate had only recently been released from jail, and the first murder victim had been killed two weeks before.

I closed my eyes, swallowing the bitter taste of the nausea rising inside me, and tried to ignore the severe warning bells ringing in my head as I thought back to the detective's words.

I will contact you once I have more questions. With your help, I'll get him.

It all would have sounded harmless—if it just weren't for his hard glare and the way his smile tightened, freezing his features in place. Back in there, when he had uttered those words, I had been sure he recognized me from the hotel, and yet he didn't mention seeing me before.

I knew I shouldn't have lied to him. Sooner or later he'd find out that Jett and I had been together. All he needed was to dig deeper into the night at the club to discover that we had been sitting together, talking, flirting with each other. He might not have seen me and Jett together at the hotel, but he only had to ask the hotel's staff to figure out Jett and I had spent the night together. Worse yet, he only had to check Grayson's files to find out that I had given him my deceased sister's name and address—wrong details.

If he unraveled my lies, what would happen next? Would that make me an accessory to murder, even though I was drugged at the club, and hence unable to recognize Jett? Who would believe me?

So many questions, among them: what had Jett been doing at the club, anyway? And how come the detective had a picture of him talking with the first victim? Why had he been meeting with her in the first place?

The last question sent my brain into a freezing ball.

Breathe in. Breathe out.

My mantra didn't help. The mere thought that Jett was a murderer was crazy but I couldn't banish the images of Gina's dead face from my head and the thought that she must have been scared lying there, alone and hurt on the street. Sylvie's home drug test kit showed my drink was spiked. What were the odds that Gina's drink had been spiked too, rendering her unable to defend herself from her attacker when he stabbed her?

Breathe out. Breathe out.

But I couldn't. The air remained stuck inside my lungs, threatening to burst. It was painful. A balloon of negativity. Like all the other things I had kept bottled up inside: things I knew but wished I had never found out. Secrets I wanted to share but would never be able to. Rare emotions that twisted inside me like worms that couldn't be controlled.

Breathe out Breathe out.

My nails bore into my delicate skin. Forcing the air out at last, I counted to three, then took another slow breath.

If the police had a picture of Jett with the first victim along with solid evidence, at some point he was probably called in for questioning, which meant he had kept yet another secret from me.

Maybe he didn't tell you because he is guilty.

I swallowed, not liking the new truth. There were too many lies now. How I wished that, for once, everyone could just tell the truth. The world would have been a better place if we couldn't lie to other people's face. I smirked. Maybe, but to be honest, I didn't care. Even if I had the answers to my questions and Jett could only tell the truth, there was no doubt that our fundamental problems would remain.

"Are you okay, miss?" the taxi driver asked when the car stopped in front of Sylvie's apartment building. He was an exotic-looking guy in his fifties with a friendly face, and hands so big he probably engaged in heavy lifting on his weekends.

"Yeah," I said quietly, averting my eyes.

I had been a great day—except my friend had been killed and my boyfriend...no, make it ex...was the main suspect. With my sister dead, make that two people I had been friends with that had suffered a horrific fate.

I handed the driver his fee, muttering, "Keep the

change." Grabbing my bag, I exited the vehicle, hurried my pace, eager to get home. I needed to talk to Jett as soon as I could.

It was dark now, the streets dark and abandoned, but compared to the things happening in my mind, the solitude felt almost blissful. As I ascended the stairs, my skin began to prickle. I turned my head a few times, but there was no one. And yet I couldn't shake off the feeling that someone was watching me. My stomach lurched in fear at the thought of Jett's brother lurking around, waiting for me behind the shadows. I looked over my shoulder once more, scanning the street in dread, then cursed quietly.

It was stupid paranoia caused by fear and the knowledge that someone had stalked Gina before killing her, and the fact that Nate was a free man again. But the knowledge didn't stop my heartbeat from spiking as I rummaged for the keys in my handbag and I quickly let myself in, all the while hoping Sylvie was home. The last thing I wanted was to be alone.

"Sylvie?" I threw my jacket over the back of a chair, kicked off my shoes, and then peeked into each room in search of her. The apartment was quiet, and judging from her missing handbag and her made bed, she was still with her blind date.

Disappointed, I sighed. In that instant, I glimpsed the pink cover of a book lying on the table. I grabbed the yellow sticker note attached to it, my glance sweeping over Sylvie's hurried handwriting.

I know you always made fun of it, but all that worrying and stress is not good for your baby, so you might as well give affirmations a try. After all, nightmares are only as real as you allow them to be. If you stay positive, everything will work out.

I snorted.

Yeah, right.

As always, she was worried about me. Only this time I worried about myself, too. If only everything could be that simple. If only affirmations worked. With a sigh I threw the book back onto the table and headed for the kitchen to grab a bottle of wine Sylvie kept for special occasions aka emergencies, but decided on soda instead.

There was no point in getting drunk. Not when I needed to keep a clear head and make sense of what was happening. After the incident at the club, the last thing I needed was to lose control over my body again or worse yet, harm my baby.

Good thing Jett was at the club and drove me home before something bad could happen.

I stopped in my thought and drew a sharp breath.

Not when he's guilty. Not when he's told you so many lies.

I swallowed. The thought that Jett was a killer was

horrible but so was the knowledge that my child would grow up without a father. While I was sure I had the confidence to lie to the detective to protect Jett, I wasn't sure I had the strength to hear the truth. It would be so easy to hear lies, but come the truth, I knew it would shatter me and leave me in pieces, worse off than before. And I wasn't sure I could go through more heartbreak. Knowing that it would be so easy to pretend to myself that he still cared for me, I wasn't even sure I was ready to even hear his voice. The lies he would tell might be bad, but the lies I might tell myself would be even worse.

Chapter 4

MY STOMACH CHURNED once more, as the detective's grave words kept circling in my mind over and over again, like a swarm of flies over a corpse. I closed my eyes in a weak fight against the nausea washing over me again. Anytime now, my head might just explode. And if it wasn't going to be my head, then it would be my heart. In all my life I had never known so little, and feared so much. I retrieved my phone from my handbag and checked my call log. No message from the legal firm. No text from Jett, no phone call, nothing to indicate that he missed me or he felt any remorse or guilt.

What did you expect? That he might just read your mind and call you even though you pretend you don't want to hear his voice?

I groaned at the thought, hating that a part of my body was so weak for him—the same part that kept hoping he was a good person and that he loved me. Buying for time, I scrolled through my contact list. It was a useless action. The weak love fool I was, I knew his number by heart, and I hated it. I sank down on the couch, dread filling me at the thought of calling him. But I had to. Even if he lied, I had to ask Jett. I had to hear it from him. That much he owed me—if only I wasn't so afraid of hearing his beautiful voice. My heart slammed against my chest as my fingers pressed the buttons.

He finally picked up at the third ring.

"What now?" His voice was cold and detached, not even hiding his irritation.

I took a deep breath.

"Jett, we need to talk. You're in trou—"

"Tomorrow at dinner," he cut me off. "If you plan on staying with Sylvie, I'll pick you up from Brooklyn. Anything else?"

I froze, taken aback by his frosty tone, when the meaning of his words slowly sank in.

"How do you know where I am?" I asked slowly.

"It's not that much of a surprise you're staying with Sylvie." His voice dripped with sarcasm. "Obviously, your best friend hates my guts and tells you to stay away from me, so she's the perfect person with whom to bitch about me. I wouldn't be surprised at all if it was her idea to fuck the next guy with whom she hooked you up today."

I frowned, confused.

"It wasn't her idea." I couldn't help the irritation slipping into my voice, matching his. "And you didn't answer my first question. How did you know where I am?"

The line stayed silent, but I wasn't ready to give up. If I wanted to win with Jett, I had to be persistent.

"Jett?"

"Same way I know where you were earlier today," he replied, his voice cold as ice, mocking me as if I should have known all along. "I have your phone traced, Brooke."

Holy shit.

I opened my mouth, then closed it again. If Jett knew where I was earlier that day, he also knew where I worked. I stared at the wall, my heart beating faster as a memory flooded my mind. Back at the hotel I couldn't find my phone. Was that the moment he had something installed in it so he could trace my whereabouts?

Surely he couldn't be serious, could he?

"You had what?"

"Your phone traced," he said slowly. "Really, Brooke, you get involved in trouble a lot, so I had no other option but to make sure I know where you are."

"Are you controlling me?"

"If that's what you want to call it, be my guest." He

sighed, annoyed, and after a pause asked, "So, who is it?"

"Who is what?"

"The guy you met today."

"That's none of your business."

I balled my hands into fists and took a deep breath. The thought that Jett knew where I was, where I was going, with whom I was dealing, was insane. Crazy. I couldn't tell him everything, not when I didn't know if he had sided with his sick brother.

"I want you to stop tracing my phone, Jett." The words were not accusing. They came surprisingly silent quiet and calm—contrary to the way I was feeling.

"Maybe."

"Not maybe." I frowned and infused as much fervor into my voice as I could muster. "I'm serious. Stop tracing my phone. Like, right now."

"Give me one good reason why I should."

Thick and fast, anger poured inside me, until the dam of fury broke. "I'm so fucking pissed off at you, Jett. You have no right to do that. Do you hear me? You have *no right* to do that."

"You're pissed off at me all the time. Nothing new about that." I sensed an irritated sigh somewhere on the other end of the line. For some reason, I knew he was being sarcastic and as usual not taking me seriously.

"What's that supposed to mean?"

"What did I do this time, huh?" Jett asked, ignoring my question. "Obviously there is a reason you're calling me, and that reason is because you're angry *again*. You're angry all the time lately, Brooke, but it's not like you tell me what you're doing or where you're going while you keep me waiting, worrying. Turns out you're just hanging around bars or clubs, waiting for a good hook-up." His voice dropped low. "Way to go being responsible. I didn't think you had it in you."

"It's none of your business what I do," I said through clenched teeth. "I can do whatever I want. It's not like we're married, Jett. I don't have to justify my actions."

There was silence, and for a second I thought he had hung up on me. I breathed in, inwardly cursing myself for being so defensive whenever we talked. Eventually, Jett broke the silence.

"That might be true, Brooke, but hanging out with the wrong kind of people concerns me just as much, given that you're pregnant with my child."

"The wrong kind of people?" I asked, incredulously.

"Yes, the wrong kind of people," he repeated slowly. "Say what you want, but I still carry a lot of responsibility toward you and our child. "I had my fair share of encounters with the law, so I know what I'm talking about. And let me tell you this: you're better off without those people, Brooke. I want you to stay away from them."

"I don't know what to say. How can you—" I choked on my words, shocked as Gina's face slowly crept back into my mind.

"How about saying nothing? I have no time for your drama right now, and sure as hell, I'm not in the mood for justifying what I did."

Faint footsteps carried over from the background. I held my breath to listen and thought I heard a female voice. A brief exchange of words. My heart sank in my chest as I recognized Tiffany's voice.

"Look, we'll talk tomorrow evening," Jett said quickly.

"But…"

"Tomorrow, Brooke." He hung up, not even letting me finish.

I stared at the phone, flummoxed.

It was her, I was sure of that. I expected another pang of pain to hit my chest, but strangely it never came. Instead, the hole in my heart dripped with emptiness, my mind spinning as I become aware of one fact.

Jett was moving on.

And there was some possibility that he might have killed Gina. My eyes fell on the open bottle on the table, beckoning to me, promising to ease my pain. I buried my head into my hands, wishing for once I could numb my body with alcohol.

I headed straight for the kitchen and boiled water to

make myself some tea. Ever since the detective talked about Jett, I hadn't stopped shaking inside. All my life I had convinced myself that fear was a natural process resulting from forgotten trauma and painful imagination spun by a vivid mind.

Today I learned there were different kinds of fear:

Fear of answers.

Fear of seeing Jett getting into trouble.

Fear of losing myself in chaos.

Fear of being so blindly in love that I didn't see his true colors.

Fear of losing him to Tiffany.

My world had become a complete mess where I could no longer see what was true and what wasn't, whom I could trust and whom I could not.

What did the detective mean by stating he had been watching Jett for some time now?

How long was how long? The thing was, even though I didn't want to, I felt as though I had to know all the answers when I had neither the courage nor the wish to meet Jett. He had hurt me so much that my heart couldn't face him without being reminded that he had knowingly kept secrets from me. And while I could forgive him for being the way he was, I could never forgive him if I ever found out that he killed Gina.

Chapter 5

I TOSSED AND turned, my mind circling around the fact that Jett was a primary suspect. My head was a dizzy mess, but sleep wouldn't come, and how could it when my thoughts kept buzzing like a swarm of flies around a carcass? The moment I pushed one irritating thought away, a new one appeared to take its place—confusing me, each one scarier than the last.

By 2:30 a.m. I was fully awake. The detective's words just wouldn't leave me alone. I tried to close my eyes, but every time I did, I saw Gina. Jett's tires had carried traces of her. I wondered if she was still alive when she lay on the street. She must have been or why else would anyone run her over when she had already been stabbed?

I shuddered at the thought.

What a terrible death!

When the clock hit 3.05 a.m. I couldn't bear it anymore and jumped out of the bed. As I switched on the lights any traces of tiredness were gone. The apartment was so quiet I could hear a bird screeching outside. A glance into Sylvie's bedroom confirmed she wasn't back from her blind date.

I tied my hair into a bun and pondered what to do. Sylvie was right, all the stress and emotional strain weren't good for my baby. I had to be more positive before my stomach turned into knots of worry.

I retrieved the self-help book from where I had left it on the table and returned to my room, then sank down on the bed and leaned back against the pillows. It was a pretty little pink book full of daily, positive affirmations Sylvie read whenever she was down, frustrated, or confused about life, which usually included the basics. It sure had done her good reading it right before she landed a top position as an accountant at a well-known firm. Too bad there was nothing in it to cover a freaking-out-about-a-killer-on-the-loose situation like mine. But maybe it would help me calm down a little.

I turned the book over, more out of desperation than curiosity, scanned the instructions, then flicked open a page and started reading out loud.

I'm happy and whole because my life is perfect, the affirmation said.

I stared at the words. Even repeating them felt hard—like big lumps of stone in my mouth, weighing down my tongue. Did I believe them? Hell, no. My life couldn't be further from perfect right now.

I feel loved and safe.

Are you kidding me? I grimaced as I repeated the words. What a load of bullshit. I hadn't felt safe in a long time and I doubted I ever would again. I turned the next page, unable to control the hysteria bubbling at the back of my throat. Scanning the rest of the affirmations, I wondered what was the purpose of self-deluding myself anymore?

The knowledge of being in the unknown and trying to force myself to hold onto positive thoughts when I lived in fear angered me. Another screeching outside. I stopped and closed the book. It was one thing to believe in a positive future, and another to delude myself. Knowing damn well that Jett and Tiffany were probably together, laughing, making love, was the last thing that could possibly make me feel good right now. It actually made me feel downright miserable.

In an angry move, I threw the book onto the bed.

The positive affirmations didn't help, and they sure didn't calm me. Time to face the hard facts, go over theories while trying to stay objective. There was only one way to do it. I booted my laptop and started to make a list in search for the worst-case scenario. Maybe if I listed on paper all my recent issues I had with him, the pieces of my puzzle would automatically fall into place and I would get all the answers I needed.

Once I finished, I leaned back and began to chew on a pen.

1. Jett had failed to disclose to me that he visited his brother the last couple of weeks. He also failed to mention that Nate was released from prison.

2. Jett had met Tiffany behind my back and failed to tell me about their past.

3. Jett had pretended to go to work while attending a meeting in the hotel conference room with God knows who on the same day Nate was released.

4. The detective's evidence showed that Jett met the first victim, Sarah, in a coffee shop two weeks ago, on the same day she died. Although I had no concrete proof that Jett knew Gina, I knew he was at the club that night, watching us, which meant he saw not only me, but also her—two victims who happened to be at the same place as Jett, and died

within hours.

Why all the secrets? Assuming the detective was right and Jett was a murderer, why kill Sarah and Gina? The detective said he had found no connection between the two girls yet, so they must have been random victims. As much as I tried to, I couldn't image Jett hurting anyone. I couldn't imagine him to be cruel, heartless, and sick.

A player yes, but not a murderer.

Except...

I drew a slow breath as memories of waking up in a hospital flooded my mind. Back then when I had been abducted, Jett did everything to find and save me—he even shot one of my captors.

Was protecting someone equal to being a cold-blooded killer?

I had no idea. All I knew was that I had always felt safe around Jett. And for some reason, I still did. However, I also had to take into account that I was in love and possibly biased. Nate and Jett's father were both convincing liars. Maybe Jett had inherited that family trait.

I tapped the pen against my lips as my mind dove deeper into the past, back to a time when Jett had tried to deceive me to get his hands on the Italian estate, a past I had tried to forget. My hands shook slightly as I jotted down the next fact:

5.   Jett wanted the Lucazzone estate, which I
       had inherited, for his family.

I looked down at the dark words, unable to stop an ice-cold shudder from running down my spine at the possibility that the last piece of the puzzle might have been in front of me the whole time; that the answers to all my questions might be much simpler than I previously thought. What if everything really was part of a strategy and Jett was involved with the club?

I drew a slow breath and closed my eyes for a few seconds.

Jett had said he didn't want the estate anymore, but what if that was a lie, a ploy to get my trust? What if, when the first plan to get the estate didn't work, Jett had to play the caring, protective boyfriend all the while siding with his brother?

By insisting on getting my promise to stay close to him, he would make sure I didn't run away, and by tracing my phone, he would always know where to find me. Gina and Sarah might have been killed as part of the club's traditions. It all would make sense…if it just weren't so hard for me to imagine.

The thought that Jett had played me caused another surge of rage and nausea to wash over me. Without wasting another second, I crumpled the paper into a ball, and typed 'Signs that your boyfriend is a killer" into the Google search browser, ignoring the last word.

I almost choked when the search engine came up with over forty million results.

Holy heck.

I stared at the numbers.

Did that many people have doubts about their boyfriends' mental state?

Wow. Just wow. What a crazy mad world!

I shook my head, both amazed and frightened. I knew for a fact that most psychos were intelligent people who looked charming—the kind of people that smiled in your face and tried to kill you at the moment you trusted them. They were in your social circles, always pretending to like you while planning for months and years in advance—like my sister's boyfriend Danny had done when he sold her to the club—the very club Nate attended.

Without scrolling down, I clicked on the third link that read, "Test if your boyfriend's a psycho," and started going through each question.

Does he have a secret room, a drawer that he doesn't want you to touch?

I had no idea. My mind traveled back to all the

countless times I had been in Jett's office. The possibility that I could sniff around never occurred to me. And when I moved in with him, Jett had assured me that nothing was off-limits, so I always assumed there was no need to check on him.

Does he seem obsessive, manipulative, bordering on narcissistic?

I shook my head. Jett wasn't manipulative. Controlling, yes, and very possessive, but he wasn't narcissistic, and sure as hell I had never seen him obsessive, unless it was about work.

Does he like to play mental games with you, where he works you up into a state of frenzy, and then pulls away, sometimes showing cracks in the mask in the form of saying things that hurt you? Does he have episodes where he suddenly erupts out of anger and lashes out, hurting you in the process, then apologizing profoundly?

I shook my head again, and again, as I went through each question. Jett had never done anything of that sort. Keeping secrets, yes, but he had never choked me, beat me, or humiliated me. And sure as hell he had never hurt me on purpose.

I swallowed as I pressed the finish button, my heart racing in my chest as the results were calculated. Finally a new page loaded with the results:

Congratulations. Your boyfriend is normal. There is only a 7% chance you're dating a psycho.

I stared at the number.

Seven percent.

That was like... almost nothing. I could deal with almost nothing.

Feeling the weight lifting off my shoulders, I leaned back, more convinced than ever that Jett wasn't Gina's killer; that there must be something else going on, something that I wasn't seeing. The thought of seeing Jett wasn't so bad now. In fact, I was beginning to look forward to it. The day had been a disaster so far, but tomorrow everything would work out. I had to believe that. Tomorrow, I'd get the chance to ask him all the questions that kept burning holes in my mind, and he would explain. Feeling a tremendous fatigue washing over me, I let hope engulf me and finally I closed my eyes.

Chapter 6

THE SOUND OF screeching echoed through the walls. A soft hand touched my cheek and my neck. Gentle at first, then harder, more tempestuous, more urgent, only to be replaced with something soft, warm—and wet. I opened my eyes. My heart fluttered as my eyes met Jett's, and I sucked in my breath.

Dressed in a pair of black jeans and a white shirt that showed off his tanned skin and tattoos, Jett couldn't look more gorgeous. With hair that dark, eyes that green, and skin that bronze, he was an awakening beauty, ready to stir everyone from their deepest slumber. He sure had woken me.

"What are you doing here?" I asked, stunned to see him.

All traces of sleep were gone, my heart pounding so hard I was sure he could hear it.

"I let myself in." He smiled and showed me the key in his palm before he stacked it away. It was the key I had given him for emergencies. "I hope you don't mind."

In spite of the recent developments, I felt a tremendous relief that he was back. Looking around, I realized I was still in my bed and Jett was hovering over me—his height both frightening and enthralling. I must have fallen asleep and hours must have passed because the last rays of sunlight were shining through the window, casting a soft glow on the dark hardwood floor. It was probably late afternoon or early evening. For a moment, I watched the way the light turned into a beautiful shade of orange and red, which I hadn't seen since Italy. It was unusual for New York City.

"I'm sorry," Jett whispered, and I turned my head back to him. My heart lurched again. Even though he was usually hard to read, I could see the sorrow etched on his beautiful face, and I felt sad, too.

"About what?"

He shook his head slowly, his lips pressed into a tight line. "I feel terrible about what happened. I had no right to hurt you." His tone was soft, and the skin on his forehead crinkled.

"What about Tiffany?" I asked.

"She doesn't matter." He lifted my chin and our eyes

connected for a moment before I averted them again. "I missed you, Brooke. I had to come and see if you're okay."

A soft smile lit Jett's lips as our eyes met again, and slowly dimples appeared.

Oh God.

Those dimples. Those lips. Those magnificent arms. The sunlight caught in his green eyes that reminded me of a wild garden. A savage garden. Wild. Unkempt. Full of secrets. Lost in them, I had to find a way out of the labyrinth. No guy I had ever met had that effect on me. Any sorrow, any pain—all vanished because of his smile.

"Maybe I missed you, too," I whispered. "And I'm sorry about what I said that morning. Of what I thought of you. I didn't mean any of it."

"I know, baby. They were just words." He stretched out his arms and his hands cupped my face. I leaned against his soft skin, marveling in the safety his hands seemed to provide. They were warm. Calloused. Strong. "Words don't mean anything."

I nodded. For a few seconds, neither of us spoke, until he stirred.

"Come here." He let go of my face and held out his hand. I grabbed it and interlaced my fingers with his. With a gentle move he pulled me up and pressed me against his hard body, and I couldn't help but notice how perfect he was, the way he did nothing and yet did everything—to me, to my whole being. Leaning against his sculpted chest, it felt so good to be in his arms, smelling his scent, hearing the pounding of his heart. To be back with him, forgetting the problems we had. To touch him and be with him, knowing that he loved me enough to return to me. Loved me enough to miss me. I had never known how much I loved him and how much I still wanted to be with him until that very moment when all problems didn't matter anymore as long as we had each other.

"I missed you, Brooke," he repeated, his thumb stroking the line of my jaw. "I missed us, but more so I missed this. Your face. Your voice. You."

My eyes felt moist, and something hard lodged in my throat, rendering me unable to speak.

"But I have to be honest with you," he continued, cocking a sexy eyebrow as his hand slid down my back. "It's not the only reason I'm here. I miss you underneath me. I miss seeing you come. I miss dipping my tongue inside you and savoring your taste, knowing it's me who can give you that much pleasure. Right now I just want to rip off your bathrobe and fuck you until you're mine again."

"I'm already yours. You know that," I whispered.

He shook his head slowly. "No, you're not. I still have to tame you."

"I'm not tamable. You'd better get used to it."

He drew me closer. "Well, then we'll have to change

that."

There was a glimmer of amusement in those deep forest green eyes as his gaze locked onto my lips, signaling that he was about to kiss me. I wanted him to kiss me so much my skin prickled. My blood rushed fast at the thought of his tongue swirling around in my mouth, his breath on mine while he held me in his strong arms—and never let me go again. I hoped he'd made love to me in the countless ways only he knew.

And yet I had to ask. Even though our problems felt like a million light years away, I had to free myself from those doubts, mainly about him keeping secrets in our relationship. If I didn't, I would feel like I was being pulled under into the deepest quicksand, drowning with no escape.

"Jett?" I asked softly and looked up, waiting to get his attention. His eyes met mine again, and for a second fear enveloped me. "Why didn't you tell me about Nate?"

"Not now."

"But—"

"Hush." He pressed a finger against my lips. "No but. Not now. Reality will catch up with us soon enough. For now, I don't want anything to ruin this moment."

His hand pulled my hair back gently, sending another shiver through my spine, as his eyes kept looking at me with an intensity that sent waves of heat between my legs.

I swallowed. If he kept looking at me like that, there was

no way I'd ever learn how to control myself around him, not when my body kept missing him and my mind reminded me of all the good times we had shared. His sexy rumble together with his sexy body and expensive aftershave were a heady combination, doing all sorts of things to me. His arms pinned me to him, making me want to do crazy stuff with him. To him. If only my nagging doubts would disappear and let me enjoy the moment.

"Don't even dare to say no," he whispered as if reading my thoughts. "We both know how much we need this. Spending so much time apart hasn't done us any good."

"It's barely been a few days," I muttered even though I knew he was right.

"A few days." He cocked his sexy eyebrow. The hairs on the nape of my neck prickled as he leaned forward until feel his warm breath tickled my ear. "Way too many hours. We have to make up for lost time."

Without another word, he pulled off his shirt, revealing rows of hard muscles beneath taut bronze skin. I stared at his body, my heart slamming against my rib cage so hard it was competing with the throbbing between my legs.

Everything from his slim hips and his broad shoulder was tight and defined. A black tribal tattoo circled his left arm and shoulder, emphasizing his bulging biceps. Beneath his jeans, he was already hard, the contours of his glorious erection clearly visible. The thought that he waited for me crossed my mind. There was no way he could be that horny if he already had sex with Tiffany.

I moistened my lips, painfully aware of the telltale blush covering my cheeks, and ran my hands down his chiseled stomach with the sudden eagerness of a wolverine waiting for her mating partner.

Maybe Jett was right. Maybe this was what we needed. Maybe this was the solution to all our problems. People always said that make-up sex was the best sex. That it could solve most relationship problems. I couldn't wait to find out whether there was a grain of truth to the claims.

My fingers unzipped his jeans and pulled them down together with his boxers, revealing his erection. Taking a step back, I held my breath. He was hard and impressive, pulsing with life, the glistening crown waiting to be touched. It looked even bigger than I remembered.

"Like what you see?" Jett asked, drawing my attention back to his voice. I looked up to him. His impatience and lust were mirrored in his face.

I smiled at his cockiness.

"Maybe," I said. "What's in it for me?"

He closed the space between us. In the silence of the room, he brushed my bathrobe aside, his cold hands instantly sending shivers down my spine. I stared up at him, naked and ready, my body yearning, pleading with him to fuck me. His mesmerizing eyes pierced through me, their intensity frightening.

"You're right," he whispered hoarsely, his eyes never leaving my body. "There has to be something in it for you. How about you let me be in charge today and I'll make sure you get what you deserve?"

With a sudden move, he lifted me onto the desk and shifted between my legs. My heart beat faster than the wings of a bumblebee as his tongue crushed upon mine— wild and ravenous like the ocean kissing the shore. I tilted my head back, enjoying his lips on mine. His hands slid up my thighs and pushed them open until my legs were wide apart for him. I gasped at my vulnerability and the sudden thrill it gave me to be so exposed to him. His fingers parted my private lips, and with delicate strokes he began to rub my clit until it pulsated with enough sexual energy I thought it might just be about to explode.

I wanted him everywhere. I wanted everything he had to give. His mouth, his lips, his fingers, his erection. If he didn't enter me soon, I was sure I'd force him to get going. I threw my head back, savoring his touch as he sucked on each of my nipples, drawing the tender flesh into his mouth. The softness of his lips, the roughness of his hands, the smooth moves of his tongue, the way he sucked my skin with eagerness—those were all overpowering sensations that made me fear as though I might just come the second he thrust into me. If only he wouldn't take his sweet time. If only I had some self-control and wasn't so human and weak for him.

"Jett," I moaned in need of release. Lifting my head, my mouth searched his, but he retrieved. For a brief second, disappointment washed over me until he pulled my knees up and his erection brushed over my clit.

There was no warning before he blasted his full length into me.

I gasped, both shocked and delighted at the sudden impact, and my flesh tightened around his thick shaft, shuddering. Hot waves of pleasure rolled over me as my sex greedily accommodated the sudden attack on my body. My fingers clutched at his arms and a deep thunder rippled through me as he pulled out of me only to dive back into me.

Cupping my ass, he rotated his hips and his hardness plunged deeper into my wet sex, nearly pushing me over the edge. I squirmed under him from pleasure, welcoming the sensation of coming undone. My hands grabbed his broad shoulders for support as he started to thrust faster, his hips grinding against my naked body. Pressing my hips into his, I could feel him deep inside my being, moving and pulsating. I arched my back and lifted my hips to welcome his expert thrusts as he rammed himself into me with powerful strokes.

My mind began to spin, my breathing matching his. My

insides clenched from the sheer painful pleasure, and from the way he seemed to stretch me when there was nothing left to stretch, boring into me as if my body had been created just for him. It was then that I heard him saying, "She liked it just as much, you know."

It was a simple statement, spoken with as much care as if it was a compliment.

My heart skipped a beat and thick waves of shock traveled through me. Slowly realization kicked in and I understood the meaning of his words. My insides clenched at his next thrust, but this time the pleasure turned to instant pain.

I winced and pulled back a few inches.

"Stop, Jett." I slammed my palm hard against his chest, urging him to get off me. He wasn't quick enough, and I hit him again. He stopped immediately, his erection still inside me, his face gleaming with sweat.

"What?" There was confusion on his beautiful face. As he took in my shock-ridden face, he pulled out of me. Wrinkles creased his forehead. "What's wrong?" he asked again.

He sounded so genuine I almost laughed.

I stared at him in utter disbelief, waiting for him to clarify, for him to acknowledge what he had done wrong. But the words never came.

"Just now you said something." My voice trembled, and

the blood rushed faster in my veins. "What did you say, Jett?"

"Nothing." Every muscle in his face tensed as he blinked once. Twice. "Why? What did you hear?" He made it sound like I was making it up.

Disgusted, I pushed him away, and walked past him. Suddenly, I noticed how dark the room had become, the only light radiating from the ceiling lamp above us barely penetrating the shadows around us. A glance outside showed the sun was long gone.

"No, you said something." I turned back to him, anger consuming me. "You said something about Ti." I was ready to fight when my gaze fell on my hand. The skin was stained red. It looked like blood.

"I don't understand," I whispered, spreading out my fingers to look at them. Shock crawled up my body as I noticed more blood trickling down my legs, and the realization hit me that someone was bleeding. And that someone was me. Jett must have damaged my cervix, causing it to open, and now I was bleeding from the inside. My hands touched my belly as if it could stop the blood flow.

"My baby." I looked up to Jett in shock. Tears started to run down my face at the thought that I might be having a miscarriage and lose our child. "What have you done? What have you—?" My voice died in my throat as my eyes fell on his awkward stance—the way he was clenching his stomach in unbearable pain. I strained to make sense of the shock on his face and the pain in those beautiful, green eyes. Jett wasn't looking at me. Something felt wrong, so very wrong. And then he removed his hand from the wound.

I sucked in a gasp of air as I peered at the flesh wound. Blood as thick as oil paint was pouring from it, and for a moment I just stared at it in disbelief. It was real blood, staining the floor, staining his hand, staining everything.

My legs threatening to give under way, I brushed my fingers over it. It wasn't my baby. The blood had to be Jett's. I looked up at him.

"No, Brooke." He shook his head slowly, grimacing in pain, as he pressed his hands against the wound to stop the bleeding. "What have *you* done?"

Confused, I followed his line of vision and realized I was holding a knife in my right hand. I gasped in shock and our eyes connected, dismay washing over me.

I had stabbed him.

With disgust, I threw the knife onto the floor.

"Jett!" I screamed and rushed to his side. "Oh, my God. Please no." Tears began to stream down my face. But it was too late. Jett's naked body slumped onto the bloodstained floor, his mouth open, his face white, his blood gathering around him in a dark puddle. My bloodied hands touched his face, my heart shattering beyond repair. Somewhere a scream echoed, reminding me of an animal in agony. I recognized it as mine.

Chapter 7

JETT

New York City, 2 days earlier

THE GANG'S RESIDENCE was located on an industrial property with several three-story warehouses clustered around a big yard, their upper floors converted into generous living space for the members. The first time I saw it fourteen years ago, I was young, rebellious, and uncontrollable, with a fury only a sixteen-year-old could possess. A sixteen-year-old, whose bastard father had kicked him out, apparently unable to control him. When I arrived money and status didn't matter. The gang had accumulated plenty through their expertise of cyber hacking and other illegal activities. The only currency was courage and a willingness to take risks, no matter how big. I took them all gladly: car races through the city, illegal underground fights—each one earning me a tattoo and the sense of belonging I desperately craved. Whatever I was instructed to do, I considered the task done. And what they prohibited, I still tried. Some said I was reckless, others claimed that I knew no fear. All rumors about me were true. If the stories weren't enough to hint at my past and the kind of person I was, then the scars on my body could prove it. The benefits of being in a gang were big, the rewards—acceptance and a place I could call home—were even more satisfying. Friendship and loyalty had always meant everything to me, even more than my position as the CEO of Mayfield Realties. I had never valued superficial relationships and contacts. When I decided to marry Brooke, I was ready to leave the gang behind for a second time. This time for real. I was willing to exchange my somewhat chaotic life for something quiet and quaint. At the age of thirty-one, I loved my friends, but more than that I loved Brooke. I wanted to start a family and become a husband to Brooke and a father to our unborn child. But events took different turns. Brooke discovered my secrets and broke off our relationship. That she ended things didn't surprise me. Sure it hurt like a bitch, but more so it angered me. As a man who had slept with hundreds of women and had enough money to buy anything I ever wanted, including women, my ego couldn't take it. With a past like mine, I could control whatever came her way. I could punch every guy who so much as looked at her, hunt him down if he tried to hurt her, and seek revenge on those who had harmed her.

But fuck, I couldn't control her.

I was used to getting things my way. When I asked for something, people bent backwards to please me. When I ordered anyone to jump, they did. Except Brooke. In life she was as stubborn and wild as she was in bed, which made her dangerous, if not stupid for not letting me carry out my plans. For the umpteenth time hot waves of anger washed over me.

It was 5:32 p.m. when I walked into the gang's community living room in desperate need of a retreat, and slammed the door.

"How did it go?" A familiar voice snapped me out of my dark thoughts. My best friend Kenny was lying on the couch, his gaze fixed on the screen of a notebook. Except for us, the room was empty. I could only assume the others were working.

The TV set was switched on and some indie rock band played in the background at a bearable level. It was hard to say whether Kenny was listening to the music or watching

TV or doing both at the same time. Ever since his return from Atlanta, his arm in a plaster cast, he had been lounging around, though not taking life easy. Raised in a family of six and being the eldest child, he felt responsible for everyone, which was why he had always tried to be the best at everything including his "career" as a hacker. Obviously he was growing too old to use his youngest brother's skateboard—an action he deeply regretted after tumbling down a slide that broke his wrist and put his illegal activities on hold for a few weeks.

"Don't fucking ask." I slumped on the couch, ignoring his curious stares when I didn't elaborate. A long moment passed during which I grabbed an unopened beer bottle from the table and knocked off the lid.

"Trouble in paradise, huh?"

I snorted and took a gulp. "I doubt you could call Brooke's latest antics trouble."

"That bad?"

I sensed some raised eyebrows, but didn't peer in Kenny's direction as I nodded. "It's a fucking mess, if not a disaster. That woman's unpredictable."

Kenny grabbed the remote control and the sound of the music died. The images across the TV set still continued to flicker in fast succession. The news, I realized, pictures of obliterating madness across the world. How fitting!

I felt Kenny's stare on me, taking in my reaction.

"Was she mad that you proposed or was it the wrong ring?" The hint of amusement in Kenny's voice was unmistakable. Ignoring him, I took a slow sip and wiped my mouth with the back of my hand. The cold liquid felt welcome. Soothing, even. When Kenny continued to regard me, waiting for my reply, I stirred.

"It was neither," I said finally.

Kenny's lips twitched. "I told you, man. Women don't get our pranks. Igniting her hope and then letting her wait for a day longer than necessary was a bad idea."

"It wasn't a prank. I wanted it to be a surprise." I grimaced and took another gulp of my beer.

"What the fuck, Jett? It's not a surprise if she suspects."

"Nothing wrong with that," I mumbled.

"Spreading rose petals on the floor one day before your intended proposal. Now that's mean. Just saying." Kenny grinned. "So I take it she said no?"

"I didn't even get to that part," I said through gritted teeth.

"Was that before or after the dessert?"

I groaned at his sudden sordid curiosity. This wasn't the time for jokes. "Forget the fucking dessert. She didn't come." My grave tone shut Kenny up in an instant.

Yes, Brooke had the nerve not to show up because she was busy walking the streets of New York City, I thought grimly. And visiting clubs. Already the next wave of anger coursed through me, this one more menacing than the last. The thought of her fucking another guy made me fume. I couldn't bear the thought of another guy's hands roaming over her body. "I swear that woman will be the end of me. If I wasn't in love with her, I'd never go through all the fucking shit and the drama."

"So, why deal with it all?" The question came more out of duty than interest.

"Because I love her." I shrugged as though it wasn't a big deal when it all came down to the three words that had changed everything in my life. "I just don't understand why she can't stop double questioning me. I'm fed up with all her fears."

He laughed, the sound suddenly grating on my nerves. "She's pregnant, dude. All pregnant women are crazy. Wait until she's had your kid, and then she'll mellow down." He raised his hand to high-five me. The anger came again, and I pressed my lips into a tight line. Kenny was one of my oldest friends, but now he was proving to be more of a pain in the ass than helpful. Kenny enjoyed any form of distraction from his own problems, and now that he was stuck indoors with his broken wrist, it was even more obvious than ever. It was either listening to other people's drama or making fun of whoever came through the door. I wasn't in the mood for either. He got the hint instantly from my lethal expression. The sound of his laughter died in his throat.

"Okay, what happened?" He cleared his throat.

I finished my beer, realizing it wasn't strong enough to numb the anger inside me. I needed something stronger, something that would burn its way right into my mind and wipe out the last memory of our fight. Kenny watched me, his face betraying his worry. I knew I now had his attention but he kept quiet, waiting. He knew better than to pester me with questions.

"She called me a murderer and a cheater. How's that for starters?"

Kenny blinked. "Whoa. Why would she say that?"

I shook my head slowly as I leaned back, taking a deep breath. "No fucking clue. I wish I could read what goes through a pregnant woman's head, but the ability would probably be useless on Brooke."

"You sure you don't know?"

"Are you implying that I'm lying?" I asked, ready to punch him in the face even though he was right. Or maybe because he was right. "Of course I fucking know, Kenny. She thinks I'm helping Nate. As for the cheating part, well—" I shrugged "—Ti kissed me and Brooke saw all of it."

The short silence lasted for all of two seconds.

"Brian's girl?" Kenny asked in disbelief, almost falling off the sofa.

"No, Tiffany from the weather show," I growled. "Yes, Ti. Who else?"

"Get out!" Kenny burst out in laughter, but the unnerving sound died in his throat when he saw my serious expression. "No, shit. You're serious!"

"I've never been more serious in my life." I turned my attention back to the bottle in my hand, realizing it was empty. With a sigh, I pushed it across the table, away from me, and leaned back, running a hand through my hair, desperation washing over me again.

"Did you—"

I pulled a face. "Fuck no." I stared at him, disgusted that he'd even consider I'd ever fuck my ex. "I would never do that to Brooke."

Kenny got up, his back turned to me as he grabbed two bottles of beer and passed me one. I took it out of his outstretched hand, but didn't open it. We sat in silence for a few moments, holding the drinks in our hands.

"Does he know?" Kenny sounded worried, and rightly so. Brian was as protective of his woman as I was of Brooke. He had been with Tiffany before she had been with me. Ti was the woman he once wanted to marry.

I set my jaw and shook my head grimly. "No, but I'll tell him." I met his gaze. He looked at me like I had just told him I had a rat for dinner. Eventually his frown deepened.

"I'm not sure that's a good idea, bro."

"It probably isn't, but I'd never keep this kind of secret from him," I said. "Trust me, I like it as much as you do, but he needs to know that nothing's going on between me and Tiffany. If I don't tell him and he finds out…"

"All hell breaks loose. I know," Kenny cut in.

There was an unwritten rule in the gang: never fucking mess with Brian. Short-tempered as he was, he loved to fight at every opportunity. Some said he was bipolar, others said it was his Irish blood that made him hot-tempered. Whatever the reason for his regular outbursts, people knew better than to challenge him.

"When did you see her?" Kenny asked, jerking me out of my thoughts.

"A few hours before the proposal," I said. "I can't blame Brooke that she's angry. She saw Tiffany kissing me and probably thought it was the other way around."

"And it wasn't?" Kenny asked incredulously. Given my reputation, I wasn't surprised.

"I swear I had no idea that she's still into me. If I had known, I would never have asked her to bring the ring to the hotel." I moistened my lips, ignoring the throbbing sensation in my temples. "No idea what the fuck's going on with Ti. I thought she was happy being back with Brian."

Kenny shrugged. "It doesn't really surprise me. She is an alcoholic."

"Recovering alcoholic—" I corrected "—who hasn't

79

touched a drop in seven years."

Kenny stared at me. Something crossed his features.

"What?" I asked, raising my brows.

"You don't know?" he asked and his expression darkened.

"Know what?"

Kenny's hesitation whether to tell me shimmered in his blue eyes. He had never liked Tiffany. The two of them were at each other's throat most of the time, but he wasn't the gossipy type.

"She crashed five times during the last seven years, not including the one crash she had earlier this year," he finally said.

I stared at him, taking in his words. Finally, I sucked in my breath. "Shit. I had no idea."

"It's not your fault."

"I wish I had known." I looked at him, suddenly feeling faint. "We met at the bar, you know? She chose the place because she was fine with it. She claimed she hadn't touched a drop in years, and I believed her."

"Obviously, she lied," Kenny said. "She's the most unstable person anyone can ever meet."

I turned my gaze to peer out of the window, lost in thoughts. Tiffany was still in love with me. When I returned, she might have harbored the hope that we'd end up together. If my rejection hurt and alcohol was served somewhere nearby, there was a huge chance that she'd let her demons out.

"Fuck." I turned back to Kenny. "Fuck! She booked a hotel room, and I told her that I didn't care for her. I said some horrible shit, and now she might be shacked up alone, drinking herself into a stupor."

"Not necessarily." Kenny didn't sound convinced.

"Have you seen her around?"

"No," Kenny admitted hesitantly.

"When did you say was her last relapse?"

"Sometime in April, I guess. We found her passed out in the basement, next to a pile of pills and booze." Kenny shrugged as he racked his mind.

"That's around the time she gave up her son for adoption," I whispered.

"Yeah, possibly." He stared at me as the meaning of my words hit home. "It was definitely before you returned. Don't beat yourself up. It's probably nothing to do with you."

"Does Brian know about the relapse?"

"Yeah. Everyone does."

"Except me," I whispered.

"You were gone too long, man. Much has happened in those four years."

I nodded silently. He was right. In the fours years I had been out of touch with most of my old friends, I had built a career in real estate, made a name for myself and turned in a huge fortune.

And then came Brooke.

"What about her treatments?" I asked, pushing her name to the back of my mind.

Kenny raised his eyebrows, and snorted. "Over the past years, she's tried anything, including weekly AA meetings, and she still crashed." He paused, considering his words. "She ran through a designer rehab clinic that cost Brian hundreds of bucks an hour, and she still crashed. Every time she wanted to get better, she did. She worked hard, and stayed sober for a while. She would keep away from the old neighborhood, the usual bars she frequented, she'd help other alcoholics, and it always seemed like she was doing better. And then bam… after a few months, maybe a year, the first crack would emerge somewhere, and the slide would begin again, only each time it was worse than the last." He sighed. "Brian thinks there's a cure for alcoholism, that she'll wake up cured one day, but I swear it's getting worse."

"It doesn't' matter now." I jumped up and grabbed my keys from the table.

"Where are you going?" Kenny said, pushing his laptop aside.

"The Trio hotel. We need to find her."

"What if she's not there and you're wasting your time?"

"Then she's not there and we'll look elsewhere," I said. "What choice do I have? If something happens to her, I'll be held responsible." I looked at him. "Brian would try to kill me. That wouldn't worry me because I could easily beat the living shit out of him. However, the last thing I'd want is for him to go after the ones who are close to me, and that would be Brooke."

Chapter 8

BROOKE

Present Day

I WOKE UP, gasping for air, my eyes scanning my
surroundings in distress. My heart hammered so hard that I
feared anytime now I might have a heart attack. I scanned
my hands and then the floor. All was clean. No sign of a
knife. No sign of any sort of struggle. No sign of Jett. A
glance at the clock showed me it was shortly before 4 a.m.
The sky outside the window was still dark.

It was a dream.

Except the dream had felt horribly real. Another

shudder ran through my body as I remembered the pain written on Jett's beautiful face, the shock in his voice, the red, vivid blood on his skin, and the stone cold feeling of the knife in my hand. But most of all, I remembered the heavy sadness I felt as I saw him lying on the floor in pain, and the realization that nothing could be done to save him.

A stray tear trickled down my cheek. I wiped it away angrily. My limbs shook as I hugged myself for support, conjuring up memories of affirmations I had read earlier.

Breathe in. Breathe out. My baby is safe. I'm safe. Nothing had happened.

It was official. Jett was not only haunting my dreams; the fears he had ignited in me were now playing sick games in my mind. I thought I hated him. But did I hate him enough to want to kill him subconsciously?

I couldn't even claim that it had been self-defense or an accident. One minute he had been speaking to me, the next he was bleeding, pointing to the knife in my hand—as if I was capable of murdering him. The mere thought of me being a killer was insane, as was the idea that I might have somehow given him a key. I had never offered Jett one, and he had never asked for it.

The signs had to be metaphorical.

In my dreams, I might be the monster, seeking revenge on Jett by stabbing him for the way he had pierced my heart when he hooked up with Tiffany. However, I knew I would never go that far in real life. Sylvie once said that dreams were messages of the subconscious mind. Waking up from my dream made me realize how much I wanted to see him and how much I longed for his touch. Even though my mind refused to give in, my broken heart longed to forgive him, to ascertain he was okay. I knew then that I truly loved him. Loved him enough that, even though he had broken my heart, I'd never want to do the same to him.

Reality will catch up soon enough.

My body began to tremble again as it remembered his mysterious words in my dream. I had no idea what they meant and I was sick of pondering over a dream. Time to get a prescription for sleeping pills that would help me fall into a dreamless state because I had more pressing issues to think about. Like the fact that a killer was still out there. Or that I had no clue who killed Gina, and I sure had no idea what the future would bring now that Jett and I were separated, and he was a suspect in a murder case.

Wrapping my bathrobe tighter around my body to help stave off the cold, I decided to make myself another cup of tea. There was no point in going back to bed. I was tired but I doubted I could close my eyes and ignore the vivid images inside my head. With my laptop tucked under my arm, I headed for the tiny kitchen. It was eerily silent as I brewed the tea and slumped down on a seat. Scanning through my emails while sipping my tea, I grew more impatient by the minute. Where the heck was Sylvie? I needed her. She was the only person who always knew how to make me feel better. She always knew the right thing to say. She could help me clear my mind about Gina and Jett. For once I wanted to forget the dreadful events and banish the memory of her dead face. Blind date or not, Sylvie never stayed away that long, at least not without texting me to say that she was okay. That had been part of our arrangement when we moved in together. After repeated fruitless attempts to reach her and sending her three texts, urging her to get in touch with me, I threw the phone on the kitchen counter, frustrated.

Maybe her battery was dead and she was on her way home.

Maybe she lost her phone and was filing a missing item report that instant, which was why she was so late.

They were all reasonable explanations—all unfortunate accidents that could happen to anyone, anytime. Now, if only I could believe them.

Watching the clock above the door while I chewed on my thumb—an old habit I had acquired during college—I counted the seconds.

At fifty-five I stopped.

Time just passed too slowly for my nerves. At that rate I was going I'd end up driving myself crazy. Sighing, I grabbed the empty tea mug to return it to the sink and wash the dirty dishes of last night's dinner when I thought I heard a noise. I froze in my tracks, my ears straining to listen for more sounds. Something shuffled loudly, followed by a jiggle, this time so clear the blood froze in my veins.

My gaze swept across the room, toward the hall.

The sounds were coming from the front door.

My heart hammered hard as my imagination began to run wild. Two days ago, I would have gladly assumed it was Sylvie. This time, though, I wasn't going to make such a mistake. If it had been Sylvie, I would have heard her key ring, the loudest noisemaker I had always made fun of. My breathing came hard and fast as I waited for the usual clanking.

It never came.

Seconds passed but nothing happened, yet I was sure someone had fiddled with the door handle. Alarm bells began to ring in my ear, and my heart lurched in my chest at the thought of a possible break-in. I stood slowly, my fingers clasping around a pair of scissors. If someone entered by force, I'd use the sharp end to poke their eye out before running back to grab a knife, and then call the police. After what happened to Gina and with Nate being out of prison, I couldn't be careful enough.

Slowly and as quietly as possible, I crossed the dark hall and tiptoed to the door, then stopped in front of it. Too bad we didn't have a spyhole. However, through the slit below the door, I could see that the corridor lights were switched on. Someone was out there, but nothing moved. Was it possible that a drunken neighbor got the wrong apartment?

I eyed the door, daring myself to go and duck on the floor to look through the slit, and maybe find out what shoes they were wearing. You could tell a lot from the shoes people were wearing. I knew for a fact that our landlord always wore dirty, yellow sneakers, which were as cheap as the guy. If Nate were outside, I'd probably spy soft, expensive leather. Inching closer, I steadied myself, ready to press my ear against the door to listen, when the space below the door darkened.

My breath caught in my throat.

Someone was there—right that very instant. There was no doubt about that now. And that someone was clearly not Sylvie. Nor a neighbor. I was sure of that because no neighbor I knew had that kind of heavy breathing bordering on creepy.

Only inches separated me from the person outside and if I could hear him, I wondered, could he hear me, too? Suddenly our door felt too thin, too delicate—too weak to offer any kind of protection. Holding my breath, I turned my head to the kitchen, contemplating how long it would take me to grab my phone and call the police to alarm them of a possible intruder, when suddenly there was another sound. A sound so scary that it made my blood freeze. It was the one of a key being pushed into a lock.

Holy shit!

Holy. Shit.

I stared at the door, ready to faint out of sheer fear. The jiggling sound wasn't someone picking a lock. It wasn't a mix-up. Someone had the intention to enter using a key!

Oh God!

Just like Jett had in my dream, except I had never given him one.

Time was running out. I had to stop them from entering before it was too late. My eyes fell on the dresser. It was so small I doubted it would cover the entire door, but it had to do. With a sudden fervor I had never felt before and not caring if they heard me, I grabbed a hold of the wooden panels and, as hard as I could, I pushed it across the floor. My bag fell at my feet, the contents scattering in all directions. I stepped on a makeup brush as I pressed my back against the dresser. It was now the only barrier, my safety wall.

My whole body trembled and my legs threatened to give way beneath me. Every muscle in my body tensed, readying me to throw myself against the door if need be.

As I stood there, straining to listen, legs apart, back tense, rivulets of sweat began to trickle down my back. Seconds passed and nothing happened. I eyed the slit below my feet, watching the shadow's movement, too scared to dash for the kitchen and call the police, too afraid to turn my back on the door in case whoever was out there kicked it in. Taking shallow breaths, I waited for the dreadful turn of the key, the push of the handle that would swing the door open.

It never came.

In my mind, I could imagine them listening for any sounds—just like I was. I just hoped it wasn't the people I had once escaped. I survived before; would I survive a second time? I wasn't so such luck would be on my side this time. As much as I wanted to scream and call for help, I knew there would be no point. I lived in a neighborhood where people barricaded themselves inside, each of them minding their own business to ensure nothing bad happened to them. I was on my own.

I wished I had grabbed something sharper, something bigger, something more solid than the pair of scissors I was holding in my hand, which wasn't much of a weapon. Maybe I could defend myself, but probably not without the baby getting hurt. Every part of my body screamed to get away and hide, but I doubted that hiding in our tiny matchbox apartment with all that clutter would give me much of a chance. Where could I possibly hide? Under the sink? In Sylvie's cramped closet? Nothing was large enough to hide a pregnant woman. And even if I came up with a good hiding place, my legs wouldn't follow my brain's command.

In the midst of the situation, I thought of Jett.

If Jett had been here, he could have protected me.

Unless he's a killer and siding with his crazy brother, set out to kill you.

A hard knock echoed through the room, disrupting the silence and my trail of thoughts. The four consecutive knocks came with such a force that the door vibrated in its hinges. I pressed my hand against my mouth to stifle the whimpering at the back of my throat. Sylvie would never knock like a maniac, like she was about to kick in the door with something heavy. A tool, maybe. I could only hope it wasn't a gun and whoever was out there was about to shoot through the door. I didn't like that thought. I didn't like that someone was standing outside, banging on our door in the middle of the night, and it might just give in any second.

Please dear Lord, keep me safe.

My heart pounded hard against my chest as I prayed, the scissors in my hands cutting into my skin.

I was crippled with fear and tears began to stream down my face. First the key, then the knock. Whoever was out there, I just wanted them to stop and go away. I wanted to escape. To wake up and discover it was just another dream. That this was real filled me with anger.

"Fuck you." The words stumbled out of my mouth before I could stop them.

The knocking stopped and was replaced with silence. This time there was no doubt that they had heard me. What would happen now?

My legs continued to tremble as I listened to the shuffling sounds outside the door. More shuffling, then retreating footsteps. Someone walked away, the shuffling sound growing softer, until I couldn't hear it anymore. I pressed my back against the wall, realizing it was too good to be true. Too easy.

I stared at the door, expecting it all to be a trap. But no more sounds came. No one entered. No one pushed the handle. No one turned the key to open the door.

It was as if nothing had happened.

One minute passed. Then another. Eventually, a door slammed shut, before silence befell the building once more. Somewhere, someone started the engine of a car.

My heart skipped a beat.

Whoever had been at the door, was leaving, and about to drive away. Grasping my only chance, I dashed across the living room and looked out the window, my gaze scanning the darkness. But I was too late. The distant sound of an engine speeding away carried over. There was no sight of anybody. No clue as to who had been at the door. For a long time I stood rooted to the spot, staring at the street below, countless shivers running through my body until I was convinced I would have them for the rest of my life.

I wondered what they had wanted. Why did they knock? If they had intended to hurt me, they could easily have done so. After all, they had a key, and they could have easily entered....

Unless the key didn't work. Maybe that was why they knocked.

Why would that be, Stewart? You think they would ask for an invitation rather than kick the door in?

The entire scenario didn't make any sense. Nothing did. There had to be a reason—an explanation—maybe one of the neighbors tried to unlock the wrong door, or why else would they leave *after* I told them to fuck off?

My attention snapped back to the hall, my heart hammering harder at the thought of what I was about to do.

"Crap," I muttered as I grabbed the phone from the table, vowing to always carry it with me from now on. Walking back to the hall, I ignored the new pangs of dread washing over me at the prospect of coming within walking distance from a door again.

I had always had an irrational fear of wrapped gifts, but after the previous night's events, doors brought new levels of terror. Both fears had something in common: you never knew what was in store for you. One push at the handle, and you might never be able to close that door again.

My eyes fell on the dark slit below the door. The lights

in the hall were out again, and no sound carried over. I groaned as I pushed the dresser out of my way, stumbling over my bag in the process, and rattled the handle.

The door didn't open. Whoever had been outside had never turned the key, meaning either the key didn't unlock the door or they had left the door locked on purpose. I stumbled back, unsure whether to be relieved or worried. I grabbed my bag, fished for my own keys, and unlocked the door. It opened with a soft squeak, revealing an empty dark hall. I switched on the lights and scanned my left and right out of fear that someone might jump out any minute and hurt me. But there was no one and the hall remained quiet. No scent to place, no sign of anyone, nothing to indicate someone was here. Whoever banged on the door, had left.

Frowning, I turned to head back to my apartment when my gaze fell on a white envelope building a strong contrast to the charcoal doormat beneath.

I stopped still as another cold shudder ran down my spine.

It was my only proof that I wasn't mad, nor was I crazy.

Suddenly feeling nauseated, I leaned against the door, taking deep breaths—to no avail. Someone had left me a letter.

Chapter 9

SECONDS PASSED BUT the streets remained as dark and quiet as before. If it weren't for the letter in my hands and the ugly reminder that Gina was dead, I would have taken into account that I might be on the verge of needing a mental health check-up. For some reason the thought that I wasn't imagining things didn't bring me much peace, because that meant I had been right:

Someone had been outside, following me. Someone had been in here, watching me. Someone had been in the corridor, lurking in the darkness, leaving a letter outside the apartment.

There was no doubt that whoever left it there wasn't Sylvie. And most importantly, they had a key.

Just like Jett had in my dream.

The thought popped up in my mind again. Great, just great.

I didn't know what was creepier: that someone had been watching me as I arrived home, waiting for me like a hunter would wait for prey. Or that they had been following my every move like a crazy stalker. Or that I dreamed of Jett having a key to my apartment and it turned out that someone really did.

Every part of my being urged me to call the police, but what if I was making a mistake? Maybe whoever sent the letter was trying to help me by giving me answers. Back at the hotel someone had left me an envelope, too. If I hadn't been told the news that Nate was out of prison, I would never have known Jett was keeping secrets from me. However, the first letter had been handed to me. This one was different—I could feel it. Who would leave a letter in such a creepy way?

A psycho, Stewart.

Another shudder ran down my spine as memories of the last hour flooded my mind. Warning or not, after a friend was killed I had to take precautions. From the kitchen I grabbed a pair of rubber gloves and put them on. I had no clue how it all worked, but I had to preserve the fingerprints in case I needed them. My hands remained surprisingly calm and steady as I studied the letter. There was no name written on it, no stamp; just a simple white envelope that was so light I doubted there was anything inside. My pulse sped up only so slightly as I opened it and pulled out a sheet of paper. It was a single white sheet covered in black, wide font. I stared at it, taken aback by what looked like a poem. I frowned as I skimmed the text briefly.

Tiny drops fell from the sky
Like tears from the eye
Falling fast and hard
Until they hit the ground,
Gathering in a puddle,
In the darkness in which they lay idle.
She dares not step in
For fear she might fall in
And get swallowed up like the tears brushing her skin
And the pain trapped within

I turned the paper over and found no name, no signature, nothing to disclose the sender's identity. I had no idea what to make of it. The poem made no sense. Who was *she* and why would anyone send anything like it? What did it even mean? New questions began to circle through my mind, as if I didn't have enough already. For what seemed like an eternity, I stared at the paper, reading the text over and over again, until the words started to echo in my head like a twisted melody.

I wasn't exactly a literary genius with an ability to interpret metaphors, but I knew and doubted that the poem was a mere weather forecast predicting that it was going to rain, because it already had been either raining or snowing in the past few days.

Could Jett have sent me the letter after realizing how much pain he had caused me? I hoped he didn't. The thought that Jett might be playing with my mind again, without an explanation, without a single discussion that included the word "sorry", while scaring the shit out of me, made me furious.

So, I considered another theory: what if the letter was intended for Sylvie?

I nodded to myself. It sounded so plausible I almost slapped my forehead for not taking it into account sooner. Sylvie had always attracted strange admirers. For all I knew, one of her exes might still be trying to win her back.

Oh, self-deception had never felt so good.

However, the problem with self-deception was that, while it could trick my mind into believing things that I knew weren't the way I wanted them to be, my gut feeling could not be switched off. And right now, it told me that something was off. I just had to figure out what.

Maybe the fact that Sylvie's admirers have never knocked at four in the morning to leave a letter. How's that for starters, Stewart?

I groaned at the irritating voice in my head.

In the silence of the room, I almost jumped out of my seat when the teakettle made a loud, whistling sound. I removed it from the cooker. As I sat back at the table, biting my thumbnail, a horrible realization occurred to me. I scanned the letter again, my eyes stopping at the one sentence:

Tiny drops fell from the sky like tears from the eye.

An ice-cold shudder ran down my spine as I pictured the image of Gina's dead face. It had been raining when Jett drove me home. Gina had been found dead with two dots painted on her face. What were the odds that they represented tears?

Oh, my God.

My mind raced a million miles an hour. If the letter was linked to Gina, I wasn't safe. As much as I wished I'd just call the police, what could I possibly tell them? That someone sent me a poem?

Yeah, right. Totally life-threatening! They would send me home, laughing. Under different circumstances I would have laughed myself. The hysteria building at the back of my throat turned into a lump as hard as a rock. I had never felt so alone and scared, except when Nate attacked me and Jett saved my life.

Saved my life.

I swallowed past the lump in my throat. The mere

thought of him was enough to send my heart aching for him. My whole being pleaded with me to get that final proof that he'd never hurt me. Even if he was a primary suspect in a murder case, a part of me refused to believe that he'd ever harm a woman. For some inexplicable reason, a part of me continued to belong to him. A part I had no control over. A part that said we created a child together, and he deserved my trust. Whether I wanted it or not, he had always made me feel safe. When Jett saved me, he created a new me. Even though the detective had clear evidence, I couldn't believe Jett would commit such a horrible crime. Then again, I didn't know him particularly well.

I grabbed my phone from the table and stared at the screen. Still no text message. No call. Nothing to indicate he was still interested in a future together or that wanted me in his life. Weeks ago, whenever we'd meet, he'd text me. He couldn't wait to call me or leave a naughty note inside my handbag for me to find at the most unfortunate moments. How things had changed. Disappointment washed over me at the thought that Jett had given up on us, that maybe he didn't want me to contact him, which was why he cut our conversation so short, and for some reason the realization hurt me more than I had anticipated.

Why did I have to check for his calls, anyway? Why did I even miss him?

This constant need to see him even though I didn't want to made no sense to me. The constant need to hear his voice even when I felt like pushing him away was testing my sanity. I wasn't supposed to have those desires, because for all I knew he could still have killed Gina and sent me the cryptic letter. I knew I should be scared *of* him—not scared that I'd lose him. If only I could get rid of the pain his absence caused me and stop thinking about him once and for all. Maybe if I sent him a text and asked to come over now...

No, Stewart. Don't you dare!

I took a sharp breath and pushed my cell phone across the table, as far away from me as possible. Contacting him again would be wrong. After all the things he kept from me, I wasn't going to take the first step. There was no point in contacting him again when I had already given him a chance to explain his lies and justify his actions. Instead of removing my doubts, he had decided to leave me in the unknown.

No, contacting him now was not a possibility. Not when I'd see him in less than sixteen hours. Not when I had no idea if he was playing one of his games with me.

The truth was that even if Jett turned out to be a cold-blooded killer with bad intentions, I knew I'd still care for him. Stupid of me, but my heart would still beat for him. And for that very reason, I hated him, hated love, hated myself for being so weak. Because as much as I wanted to delude myself, I knew I had to get away from him—far, far away—rather than seek to lie in his arms and look into his beautiful green eyes.

Heck, it wouldn't surprise me if I'd still love him even if he killed me.

Loving him was like drinking from a pond—this love would never get less, but after some time, stagnant water would become flat, infested, dirty, just like my feelings for him.

Chapter 10

OUTSIDE, THE SKY slowly turned into early morning twilight as I sat in front of the television, watching a show about a dog with severe anxiety disorder. Maybe I could get a dog, just like the one on TV, whose only issue was being too overprotective.

I sure could use one. A dog would warn me of a possible intruder. He would know before a situation became threatening or someone's bad intentions turned into imminent danger.

Somewhere a neighbor slammed a door, the noise carrying through the silence around me. Night turned into day but Sylvie remained gone. By 7.a.m., worry set in. Where was she? I had tried to reach her countless times since I found the letter on our doorstep, but her phone had remained switched off.

So when the landline rang, I jumped up from my seat and dashed over, knocking my ankle against the table in the process. The caller ID showed an unknown number. Swallowing down the curse at the back of my throat, I rubbed my sore ankle and answered.

"Hello?"

"Is this Brooke Stewart?"

My heart sank in my chest. It wasn't Sylvie.

"Yeah. This is she," I said.

God, I hoped nothing bad happened.

The last thing I needed was that Sylvie turned up in a hospital or worse yet…

Oh God.

The mere thought stirred tears in my eyes.

How could I possibly live without my best friend and our usual Thursday nights?

"This is Judith Altenberg from BankTrusts," the voice on the other end of the line said, cutting off my morbid trail of thought. "I'm calling to inquire if you're interested in keeping your account with us."

Tremendous relief streamed through me. It wasn't the hospital. It was some woman talking about God only knew what.

"I'm sorry. What account?" My fingers curled around

the phone cord as she confirmed with me the details and my account number.

Of course, Judith Altenberg. Debt collector. Bank adviser. The kind of person people like me avoided like the plague.

I faintly remembered her name. She was the lady who had sent the debt reminder. Instantly, my temples started to throb as my smile slowly vanished.

Crap.

"I know I'm behind payments, but I promise I'll pay as soon as I have more money," I said apologetically. "You see, I've just started a new job, and the hours are irregular. Can you give me two more weeks to sort out my little problem, maybe even a month?"

"Actually—" she paused for a moment and the sound of furious typing on a keyboard echoed in the background "— your account is settled. I'm calling to confirm that your debt has been repaid. Do you want to keep your account open or can I offer you one of your special deals?"

"Wait," I said, catching my breath. "I don't understand. Are you telling me that I don't owe you any more money? Is that what you are saying right now?"

"Yes," she replied, her voice monotone and patient. "Yesterday, you received a one off payment to cover the amount you owed in full. As of today, your account balance is zero."

I stared at the phone in complete shock. "A one off payment made by whom?"

There was a short pause during which I heard yet more typing.

"Mayfield Realties," she stated matter-of-factly. "The payment says 'Advance.' You'll receive a form letter from us to confirm that the account has been settled and your debt paid in full."

Oh, my God.

Jett.

"Is there a problem, Ma'am?" I could hear the sudden suspicion in Judith Alternberg's voice.

"No. I just—" My temples throbbed harder as I tried to find my voice and the right words. "I just didn't expect such a generous *advance* from my employer, that's all."

Ex-employer.

Ex-boyfriend.

"I see. Well, might I interest you in one of our special deals?" Her tone was back to its previous chirpy sales pitch self.

"Not at this time," I mumbled.

"Sure. I'll be happy to call again in a month. Since your loan's paid off, can I advise you to keep your account open to improve your credit score? As per regulations the delinquency will still be reported on your credit report for seven years. So I advise—"

I stopped listening. Thousands of thoughts raced through my mind.

"Ma'am?" Her voice drew my attention back to her.

"I'm sorry." I blew out the breath I didn't know I was holding. "I really appreciate the call, but do you mind if I contact you later this week?"

Without waiting for her reply, I ended the call. My mind was spinning, my blood was boiling.

No way.

No way!

Jett had paid off my loan—without even asking me. It was the exact thing I had never wanted. I didn't want to owe him. To make him feel like he had some sort of power over me.

How did he find out about my loan with BankTrust anyway?

While I might have mentioned my student loan at one point or another, I never told him who held the loans, especially since I poured a great effort into making sure he wouldn't find out that all my credit cards were maxed out. My stomach flipped at the thought.

Millionaires like Jett Mayfield had connections and as such the power to snoop around other people's business. If he knew people with the kind of authority that allowed him access to my private details, all he had to do was look into the National Loan Data System. But surely it wasn't that easy.

My stomach lurched as apprehension crept up my spine.

Opening the laptop again, I logged into all my bank accounts, and then called each bank one by one. By the time I had talked with them all, I was so angry I slammed the phone down, barely able to suppress the urge to scream.

Each one had confirmed the same: my debts had been settled; all of the payments stated "advance" and no, the money couldn't be transferred back.

Damn Jett!

Not only had he paid each of my loans in full, he also made sure the credit report showed all accounts as settled. One advisor had even disclosed that Mayfield Realties requested a raise in my credit score and the bank was now looking into the possibility. But the worst part of it all was that Jett had transferred more money than I owed, totaling to ten thousand frigging dollars.

Ten thousand dollars.

I stared at the number, furious beyond belief.

What the fuck!

I didn't want his money. If I had known his intentions, I would never have accepted it. How dare he pay off the money I owed without even asking me? The detective said Jett had immunity, implying that he had bought protection. Did that mean Jett paid for other services, too?

No one gifted anyone so much money, because nothing

in life was ever free.

Maybe the real question you should ask is not why Jett paid off your debts, but rather what he wants in return?

I had no idea, but I knew this: money couldn't buy my approval or an alibi. It sure as hell didn't buy my forgiveness—if that was what he wanted.

No, he had to earn it all back. There was no doubt about that. And with all that had happened, he had a big explanation to give.

I checked my watch. Twelve frigging hours. I couldn't wait that long. I felt as though I no longer had a choice whether I wanted to go or not.

I *had* to see Jett *now*, if only to talk with him and make him clear that I had no intention of accepting his money. I had to find out what was going on. Jett was the only person who not only held all the answers; he was also the only one who could put things straight. The last thing I wanted was to owe him in any way.

Ten thousand dollars.

I shook my head. I'd be damned if I'd keep it.

Chapter 11

THE DRIVE TO Jett's luxurious Manhattan apartment was longer than ever before. If I hurried, I might catch him before work.

Greeting the concierge in the foyer, I kept my head low as I stepped into the shiny modern elevator to ride up to Jett's penthouse. I winced when I caught my reflection in the huge floor-to-ceiling mirror. My face resembled a map of pain—bewilderment, shock, anger, and fear—all emotions not even make-up could conceal. It was hard to believe the changes that happened in the past three days. Since when had life become so complicated, and what had I done wrong to deserve it?

My hands shaking slightly, I reapplied my lipstick,

tapping some of it on my pale cheeks because I wouldn't give Jett the satisfaction of seeing how much pain his absence and secrets had caused me. If I wanted to make it clear that I was strong enough to stand on my own two feet and didn't need his money, I had to be convincing. Even if that meant looking like nothing—no answer, no reply, no reaction, not even a single glance from him—could faze me.

Stopping in front of his penthouse, I searched for the keys Jett had given me, and found them hidden inside a secret pocket in my handbag. The smooth metal felt too intimate, too personal, reminding me of the way his hand had touched my body countless times. Another tingling flush of apprehension crept up my back at the thought of seeing him, and my heart fluttered in my chest. There was no reason to be as nervous as on the day I started working for him. I had seen his beautiful face so many times, surely I was immune against his charm by now.

Don't kid yourself, Stewart.

Walking in, I braced myself, my heart thumping in my throat so hard I had to swallow several times in fear of choking on my own breath. But as I scanned the large empty hall, the world around me became still. All the words inside my mind—everything I had planned to tell him—died. I drew in a sharp breath and clasped my hand in front of my mouth. Shock crawled up my neck as I fought to make sense of the scene before my eyes, my mind entangled in a desperate attempt to process the picture.

What the fuck!

Jett's usually immaculate apartment with its two stories, huge gray railings, shiny marble floors and expensive furniture—the image of perfection and organization—was unrecognizable. Bright lights streamed through the large floor-to- ceiling windows, lighting up the high ceiling. I had always loved the way the large windows emphasized the grandness of Jett's apartment, but now I hated the way they seemed to magnify the unexpected mess. Rows and rows of Jett's expensive clothes were strewn across the rug and hard floors. Drawers were opened, some of them even pulled out, discarded on the floor and the contents scattered—as if a hurricane had played havoc with them, sucking everything into its vortex and spitting it out in complete chaos.

If I wasn't holding the keys in my hand and recognized half the things scattered across the floor, broken and discarded, I would have doubted that I had the right apartment. I would have thought the place had been ransacked, but from the look of it, nothing was missing.

Slowly, I slammed the door with my leg as my eyes remained glued to the disaster before me. "Jett?" I called out, cringing at how thin and weak my voice sounded. My heart pounded in my chest as I stepped gingerly over folders, toiletries, bed sheets, and yet more papers, bypassing the large sectional corner couch that was pulled toward the middle of the floor, its many pillows cut open and the stuffing pulled out. My heels barely made a sound as I made my way through the rooms, but Jett was nowhere to be found.

I frowned. I had no idea what had happened or where Jett was. But judging from the condition his apartment was in, it looked like someone had had an angry fit. With Jett's striving for perfection, it was hard to believe he'd smash in the place just because things weren't going well between us.

My heart lurched as I stepped on glass. Smashed on the floor in front of the mantelpiece, almost hidden beneath an old newspaper, was a broken framed picture of Jett and me. It was a gift I had given him when I moved in. Now a huge glass fragment ran right between us, cutting us in two.

I picked it up, my fingers brushing gently over Jett's face. I had told myself to stay strong, but seeing him, even if only in a picture, my heart sputtered.

As short as our separation was, it felt like an eternity. It felt as if many terrible years had passed. Hour after hour, I had kept sinking into some deep dark hole, thinking I would die from sheer heartbreak. Sylvie had been worried that I might try to kill myself, but how could I explain to her that there was no need for it. The heartbreak was slowly killing me from the inside, and Jett's absence was almost as painful as was the knowledge that he was in trouble and there was nothing I could do.

Sure, I was angry with him, but I still cared for him.

My fingers clutched at the frame so tightly, I feared I might cut myself on the glass as hundreds of thoughts raced through my mind. Putting the frame back on the mantelpiece, I considered what could have happened when my gaze fell on the business reports on the floor, some of the pages torn and crumpled. I briefly scanned them and recognized some client details and properties.

I drew in a shaky breath as realization slowly dawned on me.

The detective had stated Jett was taken in for questioning. What if the police broke in to search through his belongings in an attempt to find more incriminating evidence?

It all made sense.

If they found traces of Gina's DNA on Jett's tires, the next step would be to come looking for undeniable, concrete evidence that linked Jett not only to the crime scene but also to the victims. They had the federal right to search his place though sure had left a mess behind. I turned around, taking in the room through different eyes now, wondering if they found something and, if so, what?

I imagined the police breaking in, careless feet stomping on Jett's expensive suits, cutting through his pillows with no respect for his belongings or hard work. If Jett was proven innocent, would he get compensation for everything they had destroyed?

If he was innocent, Stewart. Not when—if—and that made a big difference!

My eyes fell on the open door to his office, and I remembered the Internet test I had done.

Does he have a secret place or private room, maybe a drawer he doesn't want you to touch?

The only room that could be considered off-limits was his huge office. It was the only place I had never been in alone, because it was his and I had always respected his privacy. I reckoned that if there was a proof, any evidence at all, that tied Jett to the victims, the police would have found it already. Still, what's to say that nothing was left for me to discover? Even with all his secrets and his dangerous past, Jett had always insisted that I knew him best, that I knew the *real* him. What if there was something in there for me that could answer at least some of my other questions? If there was anything, anything at all that could help me understand him, it could make all the difference whether to believe in him, or not. If only he chose to explain, but that wasn't an option so I slung my handbag over my shoulder and crossed the hall.

Chapter 12

ENTERING JETT'S OFFICE, ignoring the torn books and folders cluttering the floor. I figured doing what I was about to do would compromise his privacy, but then with so many things destroyed, he'd never know I had been snooping around.

Now was my one and only opportunity to get answers— answers I needed but he hadn't been willing to give.

My pulse sped up as I began to open one drawer after another, unsure of what I'd find or even what I was looking for.

Most of the drawers were empty, their contents already scattered across the floor. I skimmed through loose papers, but there was nothing out of the ordinary about his business reports. Nothing that would indicate he might be working for Nate or why he might be interested in deleting the legal firm's email.

My fingers ran over the smooth surface of his heavy mahogany desk. Back in Italy, we had found a journal hidden under a desk. What were the odds that Jett might have a similar hiding spot?

Sweat accumulated on the nape of my neck as I tried to push it aside. It barely budged from the spot. I lifted, stifling a groan, but only managed to lift it an inch or two.

Shoot.

I never expected the damn thing to be so heavy. Jett had made it look so easy when he simply turned it over. Exhausted, I gave it another push, when my phone rang in my handbag, drawing my attention away from the task at hand. I fished it out and peered at the familiar caller ID.

"Hey, I'm at work." Sylvie's chirpy voice echoed down the line. "I'm just calling to make sure you're okay."

A mixture of relief and worry flooded through me.

She sounded well and safe.

"I thought we had an arrangement," I said as I sank into Jett's comfortable leather chair. "I've been worried sick about you, you know. I called you like ten times."

"You did? I thought I had sent a text." She laughed nervously. "You know, sometimes you just can't rely on technology."

It was a lie. And a big, fat one. I could almost taste her guilt. Something had happened and she was trying to wriggle her way out of telling me.

"Where have you been?" I asked warily.

Sylvie hesitated before letting out a sigh. "I had a date, but you knew that already." I could almost hear her edginess through the line, which raised my suspicion.

"So…how was it?" I asked.

"How was what?"

"Your night?" I raised my eyebrows even though she couldn't see it.

"It was okay, I guess. Nothing special." Her voice lowered to a whisper. "Can I get you anything after work?"

"Is it just me or are you trying to change the topic?"

"I'm not changing the topic." She laughed out loud—the sound filled with yet more guilt.

"You are." I took a deep breath. "Oh, my God, Sylvie. What is it that you're not telling me?"

"All right. I kinda was with someone." The words came out low and fast. For someone as sexually liberal as Sylvie, her behavior made no sense.

I frowned. "Kinda?"

"Just with…you know…Kenny. I spent the night with him."

What the hell!

I stared at the space around me, stunned. Kenny wasn't

119

just one of Jett's best friends, he was also just as hard to read.

And probably just as much of a jerk.

"I thought you said something about a blind date?" I said, silently praying that I hadn't heard her right.

"I did." Sylvie's voice betrayed an edge of defensiveness. "But he didn't turn up. The loser kept me waiting for forty minutes. Can you imagine? Then Kenny called, and one thing led to another. We basically hooked up." She let out a quiet whistling sound, followed by a giggle. "As it turned out, the only reason why he didn't call before was that he broke his wrist and was in a lot of pain."

I shook my head in disbelief. Maybe Sylvie's heart wasn't as clever as I thought it was. Maybe deep down she was as fixed on Kenny as I was on Jett.

As Sylvie recounted her night with Kenny, my attention began to wander off. It was only after she mentioned staying at the old warehouse that it dawned on me why she had been trying to avoid the subject.

"He's there, isn't he?" I asked quietly, disrupting Sylvie's excited chatter, and a long pause ensued.

"Who?" Sylvie's asked, taking her time.

"Cut the crap. You know who I'm talking about. Kenny, obviously."

"I don't see him right now." Her voice betrayed that she was trying to lie her way out of my interrogation. Maybe she didn't see him that instant, but she sure knew where he was. He was probably using the bathroom or something. "Are you okay, Brooke? You sound a little stressed."

"Yeah, I am." I bit my lip, wondering whether to call her up on her attempt to change the subject.

"Brooke." She let out a drawn-out sigh. "I hope you harbor no plans of running back to him. If a guy cheats on you, you need to slam the door in his face once and for all, not open it again to invite him back in, which means no questions, no looking back, and certainly no longer showing any sort of interest in him. You have to stay hard even when pretending is harder."

I grimaced. If Sylvie knew I was snooping around Jett's apartment, she'd be barking mad. But I had to tell her about Gina and the detective's investigation.

"Listen, there's something I need to tell you," I said. "About what happened at work."

I opened my mouth, ready to explain when a blinking light drew my attention to the printer on Jett's desk. There was something about that light, symbolizing caution or a warning that required immediate attention—like a big flashing yellow traffic signal.

Jett must have used the printer not too long ago.

That was the only thought that came to mind. Sylvie's chattering instantly forgotten, I neared the machine and opened the paper drawer. My eyes scanned the top sheet.

As I read the words, a first wave of shock hit me hard.

Tiny drops fell from the sky

I sucked in my breath. The paper in my hand was unfinished but, without a doubt, the first line of the poem. The realization cut through me like a fire whip, and waves of confusion, then anger, then more confusion washed over me.

"Brooke? Are you even listening to what I'm saying?" Sylvie's voice drew my attention back to her. "What do you want to tell me?"

"Look. Can we talk later?" My tone sounded as weak and shaky as I was feeling.

"No, don't you dare hang up on me."

"Later," I added absent-mindedly and hung up, my gaze still fixed on the paper. My phone started to ring again, but I ignored it as my mind began to put two and two together.

Jett *had* sent the letter. It had been him in the staircase. He had pounded on my door and scared the hell out of me. There was no doubt about that now.

Chapter 13

"WHAT THE FUCK?" I whispered slowly in disbelief. "What. The. Fuck."

I didn't know what to think or feel anymore. I didn't even know what scared me more—that I had been wrong in my expectations of a relationship with Jett or right in my initial assumptions. I should have listened to Sylvie when claimed that I had been blind in love, not seeing Jett for who he truly was. All this time, I had believed to know him. The real him. But I had been wrong. The paper I held in my hands showed me what he was capable of; what he was willing to do.

You don't know him at all, Stewart.

The insight kicked me right in the gut. For all I knew

now, he was a Southern devil with a southern charm and the cunning ability to seduce my mind while blinding my soul. Admitting it even to myself was pure humiliation and a disgrace nonetheless.

"Son of a bitch." I laughed darkly. "You got me."

The next time I'd see him, I'd kick him where it hurt the most. If he so much as smiled, I would slap his stupid grin right off his pretty face.

As shock turned into anger, I crumpled the paper into a ball.

Jackass.

What if I had called the police and showed them the letter in the belief it might somehow be connected to Gina's murder? How long would it have taken them to find it in Jett's apartment and add it as yet another piece of evidence?

Talk about Jett knowing how to attract trouble.

After living with him for weeks, all those allegations could lead back to me and make me a possible suspect.

A suspect.

I drew a sharp breath and let it out slowly.

Holy cow. Had I really been so stupid? If the police found my clothes, my toothbrush, anything that belonged to me and carried my DNA—sooner or later I'd end up having accessory written on my résumé. Worse yet, I had borrowed Sylvie's clothes and make up. If they thought I was involved in Jett's affairs, nothing would stop them from pulling Sylvie's name through the mud.

"Crap," I muttered.

I couldn't risk pushing my best friend into Jett's dirty dealings just because I was in love with him. The thought that we'd end up in even more trouble scared me so much that I picked up a big black garbage bag with one simple plan: gather all my and Sylvie's belongings, and then get the hell out of there—before someone returned to search the place again for anything they might have left behind.

Better leave no proof at all.

Maybe Jett was into living dangerously, risking his life, breaking the law, but I wasn't. I wouldn't be so stupid to incriminate myself even though I had done nothing wrong.

Hell, I was surprised Jett hadn't thought that far when he left the letter on my doormat. After his stupid move or prank or whatever he thought he was doing that night, I wasn't ready to go down in flames with him. Being pregnant, I had to be the responsible one, putting my unborn child first before I forced the truth out of him.

Heading to the bathroom, I made a mental list of all the things I had left behind. Anything that could link me to Jett had to disappear. Opening the mirror cabinet, my fingers stretched out to pull out my belongings—only to stop in midair.

"What the hell!"

I grabbed a silver-capped lipstick and frowned. This

wasn't mine. Nor was the mascara, or the golden tub of moisturizer, or the black hair clips.

Confusion crossed my face as my eyes scanned the impressive amount of make-up, creams, and lotions left behind. They were all a woman's things. Just not mine. Ripples of apprehension crept up my back. If they weren't mine, who did they belong to?

This can't be happening.

The thought of another woman moving in so soon after our separation was too horrible to contemplate. So frightening I walked out of the bathroom, heading straight for Jett's dressing room in search for concrete proof, all the while ignoring the sickness in my stomach.

I stopped in front of the large walk-in closet, hesitating. My clothes were in there, or at least they had been the last time I checked.

Blindly in love or not, I needed that last grain of proof to disentangle myself from the love of my life—no matter how painful a process that might be. I needed to see if Jett was capable of such cruelty—breaking my heart and ripping it out at the same time as making me regret that I once trusted him and allowing myself to fall in love with him. My mother always warned me about sexy men that cheat and manipulate, but never about the guy who could make you feel high with nothing but a single glance. She never warned me that jealousy could be so gut-wrenchingly painful and unbearable, that the feeling of being cheated on could be so sickeningly devastating it would wreak havoc within anyone's soul.

It didn't matter. I had to know. With an anxious flick of my wrist, I opened the door and took a step back.

I should have seen it coming. And yet a stifled scream escaped my throat. Raw. Primitive. Somewhere deep inside me something broke, the weight of the meaning of it all, of what I had hoped I'd never witness splitting my being in two.

Arrange neatly were the clothes of another woman. Another lover—the lover after me.

Or maybe it was someone before you.

I turned my face away in pain, hiding in the comfort of the solitude around me as tears started to trickle down my cheeks. I prayed inwardly that my eyes hadn't seen what I knew was the truth, that my heart wouldn't have to accept the ugly truth, and yet, as I looked again, there was no doubt: Jett had gotten rid of all my things, and filled the empty space with another woman's belongings. He had replaced me as if I was replaceable.

Fucking asshole.

All his words of love—full of promises and plans of a future together—had been nothing but lies. He had always claimed I was the only one and yet I was no exception in his long list of games and women he dated. All the feelings I thought he felt for me were false. I had fooled myself. My legs were shaking, my body urging me to sink to the floor and allow myself to grieve, but crying wasn't an option. Not now. Not when I was pregnant and needed to consider the well-being of my child.

Pregnant with *his* child.

I smiled bitterly, wiping the tears from my face. The reality of what lay ahead of me was too terrible to comprehend, and yet faking a smile was much easier than letting the pain engulf me completely.

As grief turned to anger, I ripped the clothes from the hangers, wondering who they belonged to. Was she younger than me? More attractive? It was probably someone he fucked when I was too busy making his company money; when I was stupid enough to believe him. He had claimed to work overtime many nights and I never once considered the possibility that he might be cheating on me when all those long evenings and nights had been perfect opportunities to see whoever he wanted to see.

Was it possible he had been cheating with Tiffany longer than I thought? The thought that Jett had been too much of a coward to tell me that it was over and so he waited for me to end things in order to have a new start with a past flame was much worse than him fucking her behind my back. It would mean that their friendship had elevated to a whole new level.

The entire situation was like a frigging train wreck. I had to look even though I didn't want to. I began to touch each dress, each one prettier than the other, in search for more clues about *her*. Just like back in the bathroom, I didn't find a lot. Then again, the stuff that occupied Jett's closet now was maybe half of what I had brought with me when I moved in. Then again, maybe she didn't have enough time to shift her entire wardrobe, considering that Jett and I had only been separated for one day.

One day!

God, I hated him. I hated him so much. Heat rushed up my back as my throat closed up again. Never again would I fall in love with someone, and surely with someone as good-looking as Jett.

The worst part of hating someone you love so much is that any form of self-inflicted pain will only fuel the anger and the hope to move on, even if that meant I had to find out who it was to get closure.

I looked through the closet, skimming through dress after dress. Not a single sweater. Not a single—I stopped in my movement when my hands touched a pink polka dot fabric, and I drew a sharp breath.

There was something oddly familiar about the fabric and the way the white specks were arranged in such an old fashioned way. My mind recollected having seen it before. Someone had worn something similar recently, and that

129

someone wasn't Tiffany.

I pulled the dress out, my fingers stroking the delicate heart-shaped bust line adorned with fine lace. Maybe I had seen it in a catalogue—except, because of my financial worries, I hadn't bought a fashion magazine in forever. Maybe I had skimmed through one in the obstetrician's waiting room. But, for some reason, I knew I was fooling myself.

My heart began to drum in my ears as memories started to flood my mind.

I closed my eyes and listed to my pounding heartbeat for a few moments, but it didn't shed light on my suddenly racing thoughts and the grain of suspicion slowly settling in the pit of my stomach. A nerve started to twitch just beneath my left eye like some irritating fly. Suddenly everything around me evaporated as realization hit me.

Gina had a dress like this.

The memories came hard and fast. It had been my first day at my new modeling gig. All models wore polka-dresses while posing around fake birch trees. They all looked so pretty and the colors were rich and mesmerizing. I remembered all of it because I had admired the style.

Thalia had worn a yellow dress, but the pink one?

I touched the soft fabric, trying to prevent the next pang of pain hitting my head, and swallowed the lump in my throat. But it was too late. The thought entered before I could stop it.

Gina wore it on the fateful day she died, before changing into jeans and persuading me to have a drink with her at a famous club.

I held the dress away from me and shook my head slowly.

No, it had to be all a mistake, of course. The result of a very active imagination. Surely, it couldn't be Gina's dress.

That would be mad.

Crazy.

Insane.

Because it would imply that Gina had moved in with Jett and died within hours of it. And there was no way that was possible.

Never.

It just couldn't be her stuff.

While my intuition said there was more to the mystery than met the eye, my mind began to conjure up unrealistic scenarios. Unfortunately, whichever way I tried to see it, I was stuck with a dilemma where things seemed to be more complicated than in a spy novel.

Think, Brooke. Think. Any rational explanation is better than nothing.

Tiffany was one thing, but Gina another.

Given that Thalia had said she had history with Gina, I doubted Jett—no matter how good-looking he was—could get Gina into his bed…unless she swung both ways. But what if—for some crazy, ultra-mad, super-insane reason—it really was hers?

Answers were supposed to be simple and not far-fetched. Like love was supposed to be easy and kind. Unless I found some real tangible proof that it was really hers, I had to abandon the possibility that it belonged to Gina and just assume Jett had let another woman with a penchant for burlesque dresses move in, even though our separation wasn't long ago.

I turned my head to the bathroom, considering what to do.

If another woman moved in with Jett, she would have taken a shower, left a trail. She would have left something behind. Such as what, Stewart?

The hairbrush.

Why didn't it cross my mind to check it earlier?

With so many things from me gone, I wouldn't be surprised if the brush wasn't mine, either.

All I needed was to hold a few stray strands of hair against the glaring lights of the bathroom, and I would have my answers. Given his sex-god looks and uncanny ability to make a woman scream his name, there had been countless female employees, all of them vying for his attention, some even going as far as flirting in my presence. The blonde could be any other woman's delighting Jett for the night. If they were black, I could safely assume they were Tiffany's.

With a new rush of fear my feet came alive. Within seconds I reached the bathroom. My fingers curled around the green brush, holding it up. But there was no need. The hair strands shimmered bright red, the color of chili pepper—a hue so strong it stood in direct contrast to the cream granite tiles in the background.

"I don't understand," I whispered slowly, feeling like I was going to lose my mind. "How is this possible?"

I didn't know any other woman with such a bright hair color. Not in my circle of friends, nor at work, and I doubted Jett either. Unless Gina had risen from the dead and came to haunt him, finding her hair in Jett's bathroom felt surreal.

Maybe Jett's hired a prostitute. Ever thought of that?

A prostitute with hair as red as fire. And a love for burlesque dresses. Sure, it was a possibility I couldn't discard, but still...what were the odds?

Suddenly anxious to leave, I turned around, ready to walk out. It was in that moment that my eyes noticed a tiny, shiny bundle on the floor. It was almost hidden behind the door, out of view from the hall, but in the glaring lights of the bathroom it reflected the light beautifully.

My heart skipped a beat as it dawned on me what it was. Then it began to beat rapidly. It was a woman's necklace. There was no mistaking it for anything else. It was the same silver butterfly necklace Gina had worn during our night out, its wings ringed with small green stones. First the dress, then the hair, now the necklace.

With my heart hammering in my chest, threatening to jump out of my rib cage, I bent down to pick up the silver pendant. My fingers shook so hard I had to force them to be still as I turned it around, peering at it from all sides. The first thing I noticed was that dark brown rust covered half of the polished metal. The second thought was that the same brown stain diminished the luster of the green stones. Only rust didn't look like this, which could only mean…it was caked blood.

The realization that the necklace was covered in Gina's blood hit me like a freight train. Feeling another wave of dizziness washing over me, I closed my eyes as a shaky breath escaped my lips. "Oh, my God."

I dropped the necklace in shock, then retreated several steps, clasping my hand over my neck, hoping it would stop me from choking on the sheer magnitude of what my find could mean.

Jett can't be a killer. He can't be.

His face, his smile, his hands, the way he had touched me…based on all those things I couldn't believe he would do something so horrible—stabbing Gina, snatching the necklace, and then running her over. He was a cheater but not sick. Besides, he had no real motive, or at least I couldn't imagine one.

My thoughts trailed back to our worst fight to date. I could still hear all the anger and despair in his voice that morning when I confronted him about the secrets he had kept.

Look, I get that you're pissed at me, but it's just...complicated. You need to trust me.

What if Jett was so deep in shit he couldn't tell me? What if there was something I was not seeing?

I looked at the brush again, then at the necklace.

The poem, Gina's belongings being everywhere—something just didn't add up.

Something was wrong. So very wrong.

If only I could pinpoint what it was.

"I don't understand," I whispered for the second time, trying to connect the dots. Hundreds of thoughts raced through my mind, each one more confusing than the other. A shiver ran down my spine as I left the bathroom and returned to the living room, taking in the mess with renewed interest.

If the chance—even so small— existed that Jett was in trouble, maybe even killed Gina, would he really have all this stuff everywhere?

Surely no killer would be so stupid as to leave a victim's things lying around in his home. Especially not a man as successful and renowned as Jett. Not when he already knew he was a primary suspect.

Something else bothered me.

If the police had searched Jett's place, wouldn't they have gathered all of Gina's belongings for a concrete DNA analysis. The fact that the necklace stained with blood was left behind could only mean they had never been here in the first place. Either that or they had turned a blind eye to glaring evidence.

Which of the two options was the truth?

I had no idea but I was sure of this: the pulled out strand of hair was Gina's. The clothes and necklace were hers as well.

None of Jett's stuff seemed to be missing, only my things.

No person, and surely not the dead, could move into anyone's apartment between the time Jett spent the night with me and the time of Gina's death. Even if the letter was his and I still didn't know what Jett's intentions were, I couldn't believe he would be so negligent and scatter evidence around for the world to find.

I reckoned what I was about to do could get me into more trouble, but I felt that I had no choice. I needed to rescue him, for if it wasn't the police who searched the place, who did?

Before I could change my mind, I dashed to the bathroom and threw the necklace in a bin bag, followed by everything else I could find that linked Jett to Gina. This was an emergency.

This was what my gut feeling was telling me to do and I followed it through to protect not just Jett but the baby inside me.

I just hoped it wouldn't come back to bite me in the ass.

Chapter 14

GETTING ALL OF Gina's belongings into one huge bin bag seemed to take me forever, but at 9:05 a.m. I was finished. Throwing the heavy bag in the trunk of my old Volvo, I was grateful I had decided to drive rather than take a taxi. It was an old thing, whose annual repairs cost me more than using public transport. But as graduation gifts went, I loved it to bits. There was nothing more exhilarating than feeling free to drive anytime anywhere, no matter how long it took me to get through the nightmare traffic in NYC.

Today, however, my gratitude reached a new peak because, the next thing I knew, I'd be transporting a dead body and a shovel in the trunk.

Seriously? Was I already considering burying a body for Jett—just because I was so happy he hadn't moved in with another woman in the meantime?

I cringed inwardly.

What was wrong with me?

Suddenly hiding a dead girl's belongings in the back of my car didn't feel so justified anymore. It felt illegal, and a hell of a lot of trouble.

Angrily, I slammed the trunk, then slumped into the driver's seat and turned the heater on, hoping it would help me stop the unease bubbling up inside me.

Just do this and then you'll see how that goes, Stewart. Once you have answers, you'll come up with a next step.

It was too late to back off anyway. My fingerprints were all over Gina's stuff and I didn't have the energy or time to carry it all back inside.

I jammed the car into first gear and was about to pull out of the parking lot when my gaze glimpsed the police car parked at the corner and the two uniformed guys exiting the car.

Holy shit.

I stared at them, my body instantly hitting panic mode. Every part of me screamed to drive away, but my hands were frozen in place and my legs wouldn't listen to my brain's command. My heart began to hammer in my chest as I watched them walk over to Jett's building, their strides determined and full of purpose.

Please don't go in. Please.

My intuition told me they had come for Jett, possibly with the intent to search his place again, except I would have expected a special unit rather than mere uniformed officers, which led me to the assumption that they might have come to arrest him.

I held my breath as they entered the building and through the huge glass panels I watched them chat with the concierge, and even though I couldn't make out their expressions I was convinced that they were hard and determined, even grave. A minute passed. Then another, and the next thing I knew they disappeared from my sight. The concierge held up a blue book that I remembered was the visitor log and began to scribble.

I swallowed hard and floored the accelerator. The car instantly stumbled forward, the engine sputtering in protest. Whatever their business was, I decided to get the hell away as fast as possible before someone spied me and I was forced to answer questions I didn't have the answers to, or worse yet, taken in, just because I happened to have Gina's stuff in the back of my car.

I laughed darkly.

It was no longer just a girl's stuff. They were a murder victim's belongings—vital evidence that might be presented in court—and they now had my fingerprints all over the place.

And, oh wait, my one and only alibi just so happened to be the primary suspect.

Great. Just great.

I didn't know what was worse. That I was helping a suspect with no real proof that he was innocent. Or that Jett had transferred a lump sum of money one day after Gina's death, and everything could lead back to me, not least because I was helping him by hiding evidence.

I cleared my throat to get rid of the sudden dry sensation inside it, wondering why the heck I hadn't thought of bringing a bottle of water with me.

Oh God.

People would draw the conclusion that he was paying me off. Talk about a mess.

What if I was wrong in my assumptions that Jett was not involved?

The realization hit me hard that I could lose everything by protecting him.

I stifled the sudden need to hit the first church on the way to my destination and confess that instant because it felt like it was the right thing to do. My hands itched to call Sylvie to ask for help, but that wasn't a possibility either. Not when she'd most certainly ask the one question to which I had no answer. A question I couldn't even ask myself.

So, why are you helping him?

I was doing it—for well…

Crap!

Jett being in deep shit was worrisome, but more worrisome was the fact that I loved him. But the worst— the worst of all facts—was my stupid attempt to protect him in spite of having no proof of his innocence. It was like knowing that disaster would unfold and doing it anyway, like wanting him to be good when he wasn't. Hoping to end up back together, when his intentions could be deadly. Loving him in spite of all the pain he had caused me, even when it killed me slowly. Maybe I was no exception in his hunt for love and sex, but Jett Mayfield was, simply put, the love of my life. As much as I denied it—as much as I wished it weren't true—I was protecting him for all the stupid reasons of love, willing to harm myself by messing with an ongoing investigation.

And that's how I knew how madly I loved him.

Clutching at the wheel for support, I ignored the need to bang my head against it in the hope it would shake some sense into me. Everything I did for Jett was based on instinct, on suppositions—nothing concrete, really. Just wishy-washy stuff, where my heart was leading the way, and my mind was adamant in the belief that Jett wasn't like his brother. But did I really know him? Someone had still spiked my drink and I couldn't just overlook the fact that

142

the small time frame between 2 a.m., the time I fell asleep, and 5 a.m., the time Gina died, would have given him ample time to leave and commit a crime.

I groaned again. All those possibilities—those endless, ever changing theories—were insane. Until I didn't talk with Jett, my mind would continue spinning in a circle while my feelings would continue to be clouded by fear, making me to conclusions.

Slowly, I made a decision. Jett wasn't home, which could mean he might be anywhere. But for some inexplicable reason I knew he wasn't working late or hitting some bar.

I had to see him now, and give him a chance to explain. And I knew exactly the place where I might find him.

If Jett thought he could pay me for any particular reason, he was wrong. Maybe he had the money to buy himself immunity, but I harbored no wish of being like a prostitute, always at his service. There was no way that money would buy my silence, my love, or my help.

Just this once, I would help him out of love, giving him the benefit of the doubt because I honestly believed that he was innocent. But if I found out that he had sided with his psycho brother, I wouldn't hesitate a second to bring the evidence to the police and free myself from all ties to him.

Chapter 15

THROUGHOUT THE DRIVE to Jett's gang, I kept wondering why someone would take such great care to remove all of my things—all but one picture frame—and replace them with Gina's belongings. The image of the necklace covered in blood kept circling in my mind, rendering me almost unable to concentrate on the traffic, until I pulled into one of the parking lots and killed the engine, ignoring the guy who patrolled the entrance.

Even though I had lived with Jett's gang for a few weeks and they had accepted me, I still had to get used to the whole "gang thing" idea. Originating from New York, it was hard for me to envision that one of the most successful and most renowned men in the world had such a shady past. Were it not for his tattoos, the scars, and brazen attitude, I would never have believed that Jett might be friends with people harboring the inclination to break the law.

Long before I stepped out of the car, I could feel the cold stare from the high-tech security cameras at the top of the fence recording my every move. As I passed one of them, fighting hard not to feel threatened by the usual blinking dot, I made sure to peer into one, then waved in the hope whoever sat behind the screens would recognize me rather than mistake me for a possible intruder and gun me down.

Walking along the rundown buildings that were arranged in a "U" shape with parking spaces on either side, I couldn't help but notice how little had changed since my last visit. There was comfort in knowing that even when the world descended into darkness and chaos, here everything would stay the same: the old battered cars parked outside gave a deceptive impression of the grandness of the place. Hidden behind the bulletproof metal doors, they stored brand new sports vehicles. The gray walls looked like they were in desperate need of renovation, yet the rooms were equipped with the world's most innovative technology and amenities. The windows seemed dark and gloomy, as though no one had stepped foot inside in a long time, but I knew that at least forty people lived here at any given time.

Forty people on Jett's side.

Forty people with weapons.

I hadn't yet forgotten how much their rough, tattooed appearance had freaked me out the first time I arrived. Now my fear was surpassed by other worries. Would I finally uncover the truth about Jett and what was going on? My dread didn't so much emanate from finally getting answers, but stemmed from what that truth might be and, subsequently, what it would mean for us.

Taking a deep breath, I waited for the camera to change position and for someone to walk out. When nothing stirred, I walked along the concrete path until I reached the fourth building and stopped in front of the main door. Just before I could knock, the door was thrown open and out stepped Brian.

Gang leader.

Tiffany's boyfriend.

Jett's mentor and one of his oldest friends.

I swallowed the lump in my throat as he stopped inches from me. My heart lurched as it dawned on me that he must have seen me through the security camera and probably had plenty of time to make up his mind as to what to do with me.

So much for my surprise moment and forcing Jett out of his hiding hole—if he was even here.

With pale, freckled skin, light blue eyes, and short, blond

hair that shimmered red in the winter's sun, he looked like a nice guy until you reached the part where you discovered that his body was all muscles—the result of excessive training—and his neck and shoulders as well as his arms were covered in tribal tattoos that probably had a deeper meaning but looked creepy as hell.

If his scars and the dangerous glint in his eyes weren't enough of a warning that he liked to fight—both physically and verbally—his fierce demeanor spoke volumes.

In the short time I had known him, I had discovered that Brian didn't only enjoy being in control; he was downright addicted to provoking and confronting people. He was the most competitive and argumentative person I had ever met. I always thought Jett liked to take risks, but Brian took the extreme to a new level, which was why his people both respected and feared him. Imagine car races through the city. Hacking into computers. Tracking people. Underground fighting. Brian showed no fear. Losing just made him want to play harder. I would even go as far as to say that he lived on adrenaline—just like Jett once had.

"Brooke." Brian greeted me with an amused grin on his face.

"Brian." I nodded, keeping my voice calm and steady. "Is Jett here?"

"It depends. Why do you want to see him?"

"I need to talk to him."

"You sure it's just talking?" he asked and cocked his brows, his voice full of insinuation. Instantly, a hot blush warmed my cheeks as I remembered the day Brian walked in on us when we were naked in the community shower room. The memory of Jett's strong arms pinning me to the wall, his erection lodged deep inside of me, as the water poured down on us had me all flushed.

I jutted my chin out, feeling defensive. "Just talking and nothing else."

"Ah. Now that's interesting. I don't recall Jett mentioning you were coming over." Brian inclined his head toward me, his gaze scanning me up and down. "So remind me what do you want to talk to Jett about?"

I shrugged. "Nothing in particular."

"Nothing at all?" He raised his eyebrows.

"Nothing I can think of."

"You sure?"

"Yeah, of course I'm sure." I glared at him. "Now can we get this over and done with?"

I already knew it was going to be a long argument, which he so clearly enjoyed. Behind him, I glimpsed people gathering on the stairs, watching the scene that was about to unfold. Brian's best friends. They were always around him. If I hadn't known them better, I would have gone so far as to say that they were his guards. Cheerleaders. Fans. Group bullies. Probably bored to death with what little had happened during the day and they were seeking that extra kick, which happened to be me—the highlight of the day. Yay!

Whatever. If he could play that game, so could I.

"I don't believe you," he said, amused.

"Of course you don't," I muttered.

His grin widened as he shrugged. "You have to give me a valid reason why you want to see my man."

"Like I told you, there's no particular reason why I want to talk to him. Do I look like I need a reason to see him?" I pointed at my inflated tummy.

"As a matter of fact, you do," he said with the same annoying smile as before. He squeezed his thumbs into his pockets and waited, watching me.

I stared at him down, unsure how to proceed.

Brian was as stubborn as a bulldog, but I wasn't ready to give in yet. He had played the same game so often, I knew that the only way to win was to either give in or spill the secrets, and I couldn't do the latter.

"Cut the bullshit. Even if I had one, it's none of your business, Brian." My voice was sharp and to the point, which was only rewarded with a more annoying grin. "Besides, it's in his best interest. Now let me see Jett."

"I see. *His* interest," he mocked me. I watched him cross his arms over his muscular chest and lean against the door, his imposing figure blocking the entire door. "Now

149

let me remind you, Brooke. This is my place. Jett is my man. You're trespassing on my property. I don't let anyone in, not even when he wants it, without a solid reason. So, let me rephrase, are you sure there is nothing *I* should know that's going on under my roof?"

I narrowed my eyes, suddenly feeling anxious.

From the way he so often repeated the question, I couldn't help but wonder as to what he was referring. Did he know somehow about Jett's problems and wanted to test me how much I knew? Was he just being curious, sick of having spent the day on the couch with no action? Or was it genuine concern for his friend? All I knew about Brian was that he was Irish and that he liked to fight. If I didn't want to piss him off, I had to tread carefully.

"I don't know what you mean," I said cautiously.

"You know *exactly* what I mean." His smile was gone. My heart hammered in my chest as Brian stepped forward and I inched back. His stance was casual, but the threat was palpable in the air.

Oh, shoot.

"So?" he prompted.

Something about the way he was standing and looking at me, told me he knew something. The question was what did he know?

Heck, he could as well be referring to Tiffany. The image of Jett's lips on Brian's girlfriend's lips made me cringe. I groaned inwardly. If Brian didn't stop his inquisition any time soon, this might just take a whole day. I considered telling him to fuck off, when he took another menacing step forward.

"I don't know." I wet my lips slowly. "I'm not here to get you guys into trouble, Brian. I'm here to talk with Jett and see how he's doing. Nothing more. Nothing less."

At least one eighth was the truth.

"Nice one," Brian said. "Just answer the question."

"Oh please. As if I would keep secrets from you."

"Answer the fucking question, Brooke."

I stared at him. It was the first time he had said my name so forcefully, like a command. I regarded him warily. He was so close he could have touched me if he reached out, and my heart fluttered with nervousness. I wasn't afraid of Brian. I had once been, but that stopped after I realized he was a man of loyalty who would never let his friends down. Okay, he was a bit of an actor who played hard and liked to test people's boundaries—just like he was testing me now—but that didn't make him a bad person.

I couldn't help but think about Tiffany kissing Jett and how hurtful it would be if he ever found out. I looked down, avoiding his probing gaze, the images inside my head both raw and shameful. No guy, not even a macho like Brian, deserved to be cheated on, especially since Brian had contributed to Jett saving my life. Without his gang's help,

Jett would never have found me when I was kidnapped.

"How long have we known each other?" Brian asked quietly.

The question took me by surprise.

"Obviously, not so long that I'd know what you want."

"The first time you arrived, do you remember what I said to you?"

"That I have to stick to the rules?" I suggested, shrugging.

"That's right. You have to stick to *my* rules, which means you have to run everything past me. That's how things here work. You report to me." He stared at me, leaving the silence open to interpretation.

Seconds stretched into minutes during which I could slowly feel myself giving in. The way Brian was standing, waiting, looking at me, I knew he wouldn't cave in until he got an answer.

God, he was a stubborn ox.

I rolled my eyes inwardly. If I didn't owe Brian, I would so have kicked him where it hurt the most.

"Oh, please." I waved my hands. "If you have you to know, I'm hiding first rate evidence in a murder case in my truck. My drink was spiked and I have no clue what I did between two and four a.m. Fuck, for all I know I might have killed someone or be an accomplice to murder. Then my best friend keeps thinking I'm suicidal. And oh, did I mention that I think I'm quite hormonal and emotional? Trust me, you don't want to deal with a pregnant woman. I'm this close to having a mental breakdown." I held out my thumb and index finger in front of him. "This close to checking myself into a psycho ward to avoid killing Jett because he's a jerk. Seriously, even if I had secrets, trust me, Brian, you *wouldn't* want me to start boring you with them. I'm lucky enough if I manage to get Jett's attention when he's not busy with his work."

Brian stared at me in silence before breaking out in a loud, guffawing laughter, and then slapped my shoulder. "I was just kidding. Of course I don't want to hear about your pregnancy plans with Jett. You're free to come and see him whenever you want to." Wiping his eyes with the back of his hand, he turned to address his friends. "As if I don't have enough women crapping in my ear with their bullshit. Five bucks says she'll buy my joke again."

Someone high-fived him. I turned away, disgusted.

Men and their stupid jokes.

Typical. Did they ever grow up?

I shook my head as I watched Brian signaling his friends. Within seconds his friends, guards or whatever they were, were gone.

"In you come." Brian opened the door wide and motioned me in.

As I walked past him, I noticed how quiet it had

153

become. The smile on Brian's lips had died and a shudder ran down my spine. The realization kicked in that there was a small possibility that the signal he gave to his friends had meant he wanted to be alone with me.

That was the last thing I wanted.

Chapter 16

"SO, WHERE'S JETT?" I asked casually. In my mind, I fought the urge to leave. By no means, I was scared of Brian.

Not at all.

Except maybe a little bit, based on the fact that he was unpredictable, bipolar, and generally a scary guy.

He pointed his chin to the chairs. "Downstairs."

"Thanks." I turned, ready to go, when his hand touched my shoulder.

"Brooke. I need to talk to you." As soon as the door closed behind us, bathing us in darkness except for the weak light of a naked bulb, Brian's gaze focused on me.

Why did it feel like I was in big trouble? With a nervous

sigh, I closed another button on my coat, hoping that the extra layer of wool would make my skin thicker to anything he had to say.

"I was hoping you came to tell me about Jett," Brian started, regarding me intently. "Did it never occur to you that I'd find out my girlfriend kissed *your* boyfriend?"

I looked up surprised, but then composed myself as quickly.

"Ex," I corrected quietly. "And no, I don't believe in trashing her name. What's the purpose when the damage is already done?"

Brian let out a small laugh. This time I knew it was fake from the way his smile barely reached his eyes. It was the kind of smile that rendered people untrustworthy, especially when it came with a dangerous glint.

He shook his head. "It's strange that you say 'ex.' Jett never mentioned a separation."

"He didn't?" My voice came all croaky and hoarse while my heart fluttered in my chest while, at the same, I cursed myself for being so stupid. Taking a deep, steadying breath, I decided to be frank about my thoughts.

"How do you know about Ti and Jett, if you don't mind me asking?" I began.

"He told me," Brian said matter-of-factly, as if that explained everything.

"He did?" My eyes widened in disbelief.

"Yeah," he replied, his eyes never leaving me. His shoulders hunching and his expression hardening were all indications that Tiffany's actions didn't go down as well with him as he pretended.

"It's not your fault," I said softly, touching his arm. "Some people are better left behind. Jett should get his ass kicked for doing something like that to you."

Brian's hard gaze met mine again. "You know it isn't his fault, right?"

"What?" I let go of his arm.

"Jett told me everything." He paused, considering his words. "How Tiffany came on to him and that you had a fight. There's no point in keeping secrets, is there?"

I took one step back, suddenly seeing him in a different light. "And you believed him? That it was Tiffany, who started it all?"

"I have no reason to doubt him." Brian gave me a look as if I was the one with the problems. "If you had a lick of sense, you'd do the same."

"I see." I looked down, unsure what to say. It was hard to believe that Brian could be so casual when my streak of jealousy had broken me and turned me into an insecure bitch. Maybe I had it all wrong. Maybe Brian really wanted people to punch the truth into his face. Maybe it was his way of dealing with life—rough, without any beautification or sugarcoating.

As I watched Brian walk to the large indoor gate that led downstairs to the training halls, my pulse started to race. Not out of fear, but with anger. Anger that he could deal with Tiffany so easily, and I couldn't be the same way with Jett. Anger that I was so weak.

"I'm sorry," I said, watching him when his back was turned to me. "You have to forgive my asking, but you weren't there. How can you be so sure it wasn't him who kissed *her*? For all we know they could still meet each other behind your back."

And mine.

My voice didn't betray the bitterness of thousands of needles poking into my heart at the memory of Tiffany's voice on the phone. She had been there with him. Who knew what they had been doing the day before, when Jett cut me off? Behind my eyes, I could feel the dreadful swelling of gathering tears. Even knowing about their past felt painful, and knowing that she still was close to Jett, might be kissing him that instant, sleeping with him. Had a child with him.

"That's an easy one." Brian avoided my probing gaze as he typed in the code. A brief, low sound echoed as the red light changed to green, and the gate opened. With a blank expression, Brian turned to me, motioning me to enter. "Jett said you've been here before. So I'm thinking I can rely on you as a point of reference, right?"

Was he just asking me if Jett was telling the truth? I stared at him, unsure, faced with the fact that I kept hearing double-meanings. "Are you asking me?"

"Yes."

"That part is true, yes," I said slowly, blinking away the tears. "I saw them kissing before I left. And yes, she might have started it. But still, it doesn't change the fact that they met behind our backs, Brian. What's to say they weren't having an affair for weeks or months and we were clueless?"

What was to say they weren't still?

My voice sounded so stricken, he eyed me in silence for a few moments.

"Were you in a relationship with Jett when they kissed?" Brian asked eventually.

"What's that got to do with it?" I asked, frowning.

"Everything," he replied. "I know Tiff. And I know Jett. And the only thing you need to know is that Jett isn't a cheater." He took a few steps toward me, his blue eyes looking at me in thought. In the narrow hall, his tall figure seemed to swallow up the entire space. "Jett has made some mistakes but I don't think he ever cheated on anyone, Brooke. He's as faithful and loyal as anyone can be. It's part of the reason why I let him return to my gang. I knew I could trust his word." He raised his eyebrows as if to convey the importance of his words. "Let's face it. Trust is

159

much harder to find than the next girlfriend. And Jett has always been a loyal dog. Tiffany on the other side—" he paused and something dark and menacing crossed his features "—she always does what she wants when she's drunk. If she hadn't been honest about her problems, I would have kicked her out of here a long time ago."

I cringed at her name.

Tiffany.

Bitch.

The thought that she was still living here drove me mad. Her being under the same roof as Jett made my blood boil. I hated her so much. Without her, I would have never ended things with Jett. In spite of any problems, I would have worked things out with him. Or at least I would have tried.

"So you knew all along." The question was meant to be a statement and yet my tone came out accusatory. All the hurt started to seep through, and there was nothing I could do about that.

"Yeah, I did. I know all about her feelings for Jett."

I stared at him in disbelief. "If you already knew, why did you ask me then? Is this some sort of sick joke to you?"

"Obviously to see if you're lying. I'm not stupid, you know." He caught my hard glance and returned it. "Maybe she believes she's in love with him, but it doesn't change the fact that he was always just a rebound and she's an alcoholic. And Jett knows—better than anyone—that he can't take her seriously."

"What are you saying?" I asked, confused by the direction our conversation was taking.

"The kiss. What you assume is cheating. Drinking clouds her feelings, it changes her character." He sighed, his gaze wandering to his black military shoes. "It's happened before. A lot of times, and not just with Jett. It was just a matter of time until it happened again. So yes, you could say that I saw it coming. But then she's an alcoholic."

"And that's supposed to make me feel better and forgive her?" I asked sourly.

"I don't expect you to do anything." He looked up. "But I hope you don't let it jeopardize your relationship with Jett just because she made a mistake."

"I'm not jeopardizing…" I trailed off.

I did, or at least had done.

I had blamed him. Fully, without a single doubt.

"Just saying." He cocked his eyebrow, and then he moved past me, calling over his shoulder, "You'll find him downstairs. If you can get him to stop his madness that he calls training, so that I can finally get a couple hours of sleep, tell him that'd be grand."

I frowned, wondering what he meant by that, but didn't care to ask.

"You're welcome to stay as long as you want," Brian

continued. "We have plenty of rooms available in building five."

I snorted. "You mean, if things don't work out with Jett."

He chuckled. "It was only a suggestion. Doesn't mean Jett will let you stay in any of them"

"You mean here with him?"

Brian shook his head slowly, an amused glint playing in his eyes. "No, over there. In building five."

I stared at him. Building five, or more precisely warehouse five, housed five others. All of them male. All of them single. I slowly got his drift.

"There's no need for that," I said.

"Good." He was gone before I could utter another word, leaving me in the darkness of the hall.

Chapter 17

ALL MY LIFE I had watched people fall in love. The thing was, I had never expected to fall so hard myself—that plunging into complete darkness, with nothing but a trusting heart that meant I had to stop breathing to allow for someone's breath to become mine. Ever since Jett's lips had touched mine, I felt as though I was branded. I felt like a part of me had died, rising from the ashes, only to become a part of him. Maybe love was a pink witch, on the outside a pretty face bewitching us, blinding us, and on the inside—behind its mask—rearing its ugly head, trapping us with its charming spell, forcing us into a state of obsession and lust-fueled madness where obsession became my reality.

As I stepped down the stairs and opened the last door to the large training halls, a large subterranean maze complete with a boxing ring and training equipment, my eyes fell on the lonely figure, and my heart died and cheered at the same time. That instant, all the questions I had wanted to ask vanished.

This was real.

This was really happening.

Seeing Jett after all the drama and confusing dream felt surreal. Like losing a favorite possession and being reunited with it years later, then having to gawk at it from afar, unable to grasp it in your hands.

Except Jett wasn't standing that far away.

He was close—too close, like the sky touching the clouds, the sound of him punching the bag the only noise echoing through the hall. It was strange how one minute you thought everything mattered, and then with one single glance, everything became nothing, except for that one guy, who could make you fall in love with him over and over again, day after day, in just a heartbeat.

An unwanted smile spread across my lips.

Despite everything—the drama, the secrets, the danger, and most of all the possibility he might be a killer—his perfect body still excited me. Too bad his character wasn't perfect, and I was a romantic with a weak spot for tattooed Southern guys. Jett looked angry, but more so he looked so damn sexy, I couldn't help but run the tip of my tongue over my lips. If it weren't for our much-needed conversation, I would have chosen to stand there the entire day, watching him and daydream about all the naughty things I'd do with him.

Get a grip! He's a bad boy.

A bad boy with a talent for creating pleasure.

It was hard to resist a bad boy who might be good for my body but not for my heart.

In the darkness of the room, I stood and watched his lean, half-naked body, each muscle straining as he hit the huge black punching bag hard, over and over again. A layer of sweat covered his back and forehead. His bulging biceps strained as he punched the bag, his muscles flexing beneath the tan skin. I was about to admire his strong thighs when I noticed his shins were all blue and bruised. I wondered how long he had been training. All morning? All night? No wonder Brian asked me to stop "his madness."

"Jett?" I said quietly, stopping at a safe distance. His face a mask of concentration and focus, he looked so engrossed in what he was doing I doubted he had heard me. The way he kept slamming his hurt leg into the punching bag faster and harder I was sure that either one—leg or the bag— would break soon.

"Jett!" I shouted to get his attention.

He stopped and whirled around. Confusion crossed his

face, and then the swinging bag hit him and he stumbled backward, but only so slightly.

"Brooke?" he asked, his hands stopping the bag from swinging again, his eyes never leaving mine. The surprise was written on his face as his gaze scanned over me as if he could not believe it was me standing in front of him.

"What are you doing?" I asked shocked, glancing at the blue specks covering his leg and the blood-soaked bandages that covered his knuckles. "You're completely bruised and bleeding."

My stomach fluttered as I watched him come closer. He was so tall. So strong. His face both beautiful and haunting, with glinting green eyes, and hair so dark, he would be my downfall. Blood had begun to seep through the bandages covering his knuckles, and his shins shimmered bluish beneath his skin.

He caught my glance on his hand.

"It's supposed to look this way," he replied to my unspoken question.

"Not like this."

He shook his head grimly. "That's nothing. I'm used to worse."

Silence ensued. I knew I had to talk, fill the void of communication, but suddenly my prepared speech was gone.

It had been so much easier in my imagination, in my

dreams, in my plans. I would have asked him questions, he would give me answers, and then I would move on. Or not, but it was as simple as that.

However, standing in front of him, with him watching me, I grew nervous. I didn't know where to start, what to do or say. He wasn't supposed to look mortally wounded. He wasn't supposed to look so sexy and delicious half-naked, making me forget all the things I needed to get off my chest. Fuck, he wasn't allowed to be so sinfully irresistible, making my body want to touch him when I should be mad at him.

Before I could stop myself, my fingers stroked over his bruised knuckles, and a soft shiver ran through me. "We need to get it looked at before it gets infected, you know?" I murmured, avoiding his eyes. "If you tell me where the first aid kit is, I'll get this disinfected in no time."

"Why are you here, Brooke?" His voice was low and flat but carried an unmistakable hint of anger.

I swallowed hard.

When Brian asked me what I was doing here, I thought it was out of curiosity. I knew he'd try to test me. This felt different. Unlike with Brian, I felt like I had everything to lose with Jett. I felt like I was stepping over boundaries—onto territory where I felt vulnerable. Exposed, with my insides open for everyone to see. For some reason, him not wanting to see me hurt me more than I thought it would.

He was angry with me—I got that—but so was I with him for even asking this question.

"What do you think I am doing here?" I asked, but the words didn't sound as accusing as I'd intended. "You paid off my loans. I don't need your fucking money, Jett. I don't need handouts. I'm perfectly capable of paying off the money I own on my own."

It was a lie.

One he would know if he had indeed checked my balance.

Towering over me, his gaze lingered on me too long. His jaw was tight—the way it often was when he was trying to control himself. I knew then that he wasn't happy to see me. That he really had no idea why I was here, and that the silence between us felt awkward.

"Forget it. It was a bad idea to come here, seeing that you didn't even want to see me. Just do me the favor and take the money back. I don't want it, and I don't want to have anything to do with it." Turning my back to him, I was ready to walk out the room when his hand grabbed my elbow, stopping me in my movement.

I swallowed hard, marveling at the strong feel of his grip.

"I know you would have paid them off eventually. There was never a doubt about it," he murmured so low I wasn't sure I heard him. "It's not a handout, though,

Brooke. It's what I owe you."

I turned back to him, taking in his posture. The expression on his face had softened; the hard grip on my elbow was gone. My whole body began to tense because of the way he kept looking at me—his eyes warm and yet his mouth hard, his half-naked body urging me to touch him, his breath asking me to kiss him, and yet I knew that wasn't an option.

I would never allow it.

Not now. Not ever, Stewart.

"I don't understand," I muttered.

"Consider it an advance payment rather than money borrowed," Jett said coolly.

"For what?"

"I made you partner at Mayfield Realties," he said, his eyes glimmering with something I couldn't quite pinpoint.

I almost tripped in my high heels. The realization of what he had just said kicked in and ever so slowly my mouth dropped open.

He made me partner in his business?

Holy cow!

Why the heck would he do that?

"What?" I stared at him in shock.

Hundreds of thoughts raced through my mind, flying so fast I wasn't able to catch my breath. I shook my head in confusion. Did I miss something? Did I misinterpret his

169

tone of anger from before?

"I don't understand," I said in disbelief. "Why would you make me partner?"

"What do you mean 'why?'" The skin around his stunning eyes crinkled ever so softly, but other than that his face remained a mask of nonchalance. "Why does there always have to be a why with you? Isn't it enough that I'm confident in your skills and that you have good references?"

That happens when you sleep with the boss, Stewart.

"References?" I raised my eyebrows. "Yours, I assume?"

"That's right." Now, was that another hint of amusement I detected?

I shook my head, letting out a slow breath. "Jett, I can't lead a whole company. Not even half of it. That's just crazy," I said, shaking my head again. "I'm sure it's some people's dream to make it partner. You'll probably find plenty of them on the board, people more suited to this position. Steve, for example. He's been waiting for a promotion for years. Or you could choose Colt."

"Steve's a two-sided snake and you know that. And Colt is way too old. He wants to retire." He smiled that lopsided smile of his that always managed to send my pulse racing. "You, in turn, are young. Straightforward. Honest. Perfect as *my* partner."

His partner. My breath hitched in my throat.

Holy mother of double meanings!

I stared at him, not quite trusting his words when one minute we were having a fight, and the next he had promoted me. Something just didn't add up.

There had to be some motive—some ulterior motive I wasn't seeing.

I narrowed my eyes as I let my gaze sweep over his perfect features. "Why would you make me partner, Jett?" I asked, not hiding my mistrust.

"You earned it, Brooke." He inched closer until he stood mere inches away. He was so close I could smell his manly scent that screamed of power, tenacity and sexiness—of the intoxicating kind—and I realized it must be his scent that made it so hard to think clearly. The knowledge he was a fighter of the hard kind. A sex god, who just had to remove his shirt to make my panties wet. Or maybe it was the feel of his hands going around my waist, pulling me slowly to him until I could feel nothing but the heat emanating from his body.

He pulled me closer and the room began to spin.

Slowly, my bitterness began to fade away, which angered me. Anger was all I had to keep me away from him—both physically and emotionally. Anger was a necessary ingredient for helping me focus on the future, let go of bygones, and move on.

Or at least make sense of everything.

Without it, I would succumb and plead with him to take

me right there and then.

"It would make me happy to see you in this position," Jett said hoarsely.

"I can't accept it, Jett," I whispered weakly just when his hands traveled down my back, lingering, threatening to brush over my ass. "It's a huge responsibility, not to mention a risk. I don't want to be the one who…"

"I'm not taking 'no' for an answer," he cut me off and his eyes met mine. "You're the only one I trust in my company. If anyone should be partner, I want it to be you."

"What about the risks? Are you willing to take those?"

"There won't be any," he said. "And besides, with great risk comes great success. You're worth it. I know you have what it takes to succeed."

Help Jett lead his new company? That was crazy. And yet the thought of working close to him, of being near, made my heart beat faster. Working in real estate had always been my dream. The prospect of being around the man of my dreams all the time felt like heaven. It was almost perfect—except for the secrets he had yet to reveal to me.

I tensed.

Secrets.

Ugly secrets that managed to ruin any mood. Dark secrets that kept us from building trust. I hated them with ferocity. Hated that they so easily covered everything positive in our lives, until nothing was left.

Looking into his face, I wanted to forgive him, not least because I needed some great make-up sex. But that wasn't an option until he cleared my doubts.

If he'd just tell me what was going on, confirm that he hadn't killed Gina, I knew I could start to forgive him. For a moment panic rose within me as I remembered how much we had to clear—so much it felt like it could take all day.

Good gracious.

"It's already done," Jett said, his hand still stroking my back. "I've announced the news to the board and you're expected to start next week. As of Tuesday, you'll commence your new position. I'm putting every faith in you, Brooke."

Time was running out. There was no doubt. Jett had to tell me everything. He had to clarify, but Jett wasn't exactly an open book. I took a deep breath, wondering how the heck I could help him open up to me when I had tried before and miserably failed.

"Why are you so sure I want to work with you after all the secrets you've been keeping?" I asked.

The pause only lasted two seconds.

"Because I will ask you to." His voice dropped to a whisper, his hand pulling my hair back. "Colt will get you all the training and everything else you need, though to be honest, I think you'll do just fine."

"You make it sound like I'm doing it all on my own." It was meant to be a joke…until I noticed the tiny twitch beneath his eye and my smile died on my lips.

"What?"

He drew a sharp breath, pausing a little, then exhaling slowly.

"Brooke, there's a reason why I promoted you. Why I insisted you worked as a project manager and as my assistant. It was so that I could teach you the ins and outs of this company." My pulse spiked—and not in a good way. There was something in his tone that wasn't in tune with what he was saying. His expression was so soft, and yet there was a hard edge in his eyes. And I didn't like it. Jett had never regarded me with this kind of hard stare. Suddenly I could feel him tense.

"I'm moving to Chicago," he said at last, the words cutting through the air like a knife.

I froze.

He's moving.

The words kept echoing inside my brain. If Jett made me partner in his real estate business in New York City and he moved to Chicago that would mean we'd be no longer seeing each other.

There would be no us anymore because long-distance relationships hardly ever worked out.

"You're moving to Chicago?" I asked in disbelief.

"That's right," he whispered. "We won't be seeing each other for some time."

For some time.

Oh, my God.

Oh. My. God.

My throat tightened and my knees threatened to collapse beneath me—like a house of cards.

He made you partner. Sounds like a pity move, Stewart. A goodbye gift.

Maybe even an attempt to pay me off.

Get rid of me.

"For how long?" I sounded so choked I could only hope that he could hear me.

"As long as it takes."

"What sort of crappy answer is that, Jett? For how long?"

He shrugged, not even caring to look at me. "It might be months. Maybe a couple of years. Who knows?"

"What about the baby? You're going to miss its birth."

"*You're* going to raise it." His jaw set. "That's just how things are."

My eyes moistened again. All my fears, my nightmares— they were real. I was going to kill him, because he had just killed me with his words.

Bastard!

After everything we had been through, he was going to leave me—pregnant, clueless, and heartbroken.

The statement hit me like a train. He was trying to break up with me, for real. Trying to move on. Start a new life. Miss the birth of his child. He had never had the intention to reconcile or start a family, to be there for his child. That was the reason why he didn't tell me about Nate's release, why he had kept all his secrets. He didn't care about me. Hurt and anger poured through me in thick, heavy waves. Tears started to spill from my eyes. My breath came hard and heavy. Suddenly his arms felt like needles. Painful. Raw. Sharp. I pushed him away, the pain threatening to kill me.

"When were you going to tell me?" My voice increased in volume.

His lips pressed into a tight line, he turned his back to me. It was the Jett I knew—turning his back on me, refusing to give answers. I stared at his back, shocked by his reluctance to explain or try to ease my pain, as he ambled over to a huge bucket filled with ice cubes and stopped in front of it.

"Answer the question, Jett." I walked after him. "How long have you known?"

My voice shook as I tried to regain control of the raging storm inside me.

In the silence of the room I watched him remove the bandages from his knuckles. They looked sore, but I couldn't have cared less. I couldn't have cared less if he cut himself or if he was bleeding. Avoiding my gaze, Jett remained silent as he grabbed a few ice cubes from the huge bucket, then wrapped the bandages around them and pressed them against his skin. The seconds stretched into minutes. When he finally raised his head, his eyes were cold and his face emotionless.

"I'm sorry, Brooke. I can't tell you more than I have," he said, turning his attention back to his hand, repeating the words he had said before, "That's just the way things are right now. Nothing can change my decision."

Chapter 18

I STARED AT him in shock, feeling like I was about to explode from the inside. My hands trembled. Anytime now, the agony inside my chest would break me. I didn't just know; I was sure of it. Looking at Jett, at the way his eyes couldn't even look at me, at the way his mouth was set, I felt the pain deep inside my heart and knew I had only two choices:

Break or get broken.

The pain I felt in my heart was more intense, rawer, and deeper than any emotion I had ever experienced before. If I didn't do anything right now—anything at all to stop the pain—it would kill me. It sure felt like I was dying from the inside, the seconds slowly ticking like a bomb.

Without thinking, I stepped in front of the bucket and with a brutal force I had stored for too long, I plunged my hand into the ice. Instant pain soared up my arm as the sharp clusters of ice cubes broke through the delicate skin of my fingers. Pulling my hand out, the aching shot straight up my arms.

But I didn't care.

By going away, he would leave me and my child behind with no chance to mend what was broken, what I hoped could be reconciled. He would leave my future bleak. Sure, he had secrets, sure his words had hurt me, but I loved him nonetheless.

I pushed my hand back into the bucket again, diving a little deeper until I was sure I was bleeding, and the ice started to both burn and numb my skin at the same time. In spite of the stinging tears and the strange tightening sensation in my chest, the numbness in my hands felt different. It was oddly comforting and anesthetizing. Much more tolerable than the pain Jett had caused me.

"Stop it, Brooke. You're going to hurt yourself," Jett said.

"I don't care. It's my body."

"Don't be stupid," he roared. "You're pregnant."

"Why do you care? Don't you have a suitcase to pack or something?" I pulled my hands out only to shove them back in again.

"Stop it." He had stepped next to me, watching me in both anger and shock. "You're fucking hormonal and emotional."

Seriously?

Now he was blaming my pregnancy for his failings.

Yes, I was emotional, but *I was not* hormonal. At least not a lot. Not that it affected me, or did it? Who cared?

"Nice try." I let out a laugh. "Now you blame my pregnancy when it's in fact your fault that I'm reacting this way."

His eyes narrowed on me. "Hold on. How is it my fault?"

"After what you just said, how can you still pretend it's not your fault, Jett?" I stared at him, full of contempt. "There's no reason for you to lie anymore, so stop pretending and just be honest." I ground my hand against the ice, enjoying the painful sensation.

"Stop it, Brooke."

"Says the one who kicked his shins bloody."

I readied myself to thrust my hands back in again, when he grabbed my hand, holding it up in midair.

"I said, *stop it.*" His deep voice didn't leave room for discussion.

"Why do the fuck do you care?" I repeated.

"Because I just do." He tightened his grip on my hand.

"The fuck you are. Let go of me." As hard as I could I

pulled my hand away, but his hold on me remained relentless.

"I will when you've calmed yourself."

"Calm myself?" I laughed. "I'm fucking calm."

"No, you're not."

He was right. I wasn't.

All those hormones rushing inside of me felt crushing. They might be pregnancy hormones. They might be stress hormones caused by insomnia. Whatever. I didn't care what they were called.

"You've no right," I hissed, yanking my hand again. "No right to tell me what to do. My life, my body, my choices, my mistakes, they are not your problems. Not your business."

I had every intention of continuing to slam my hand into the sharp ice—until my heart stopped breaking. It was either my heart or my hand. And my hand had to do.

For once I was grateful that Sylvie had dragged me to a training course years ago where I had learned how to deal with situations like this. Twisting my hand out of Jett's tight grip, I pushed him away and was about to start to punch the ice again when something gripped me from behind.

It was Jett.

The movement of him wrapping his strong arms around me came so unexpected it knocked my breath out of my lungs as he lifted me up in the air.

For a moment I was stunned, and then I started struggling against his iron grip.

It wasn't possible.

My feet dangled up in the air, and judging from the lock on my body, he had no intention of letting go of me.

"Let me down!" I screamed.

An amused snort escaped his lips, infuriating me even more as he carried me away from the bucket of ice cubes like I weighed nothing. I struggled, but my attempts to escape were fruitless. Jett had me on lockdown.

More anger washed over me, threatening to burn me like fire. How the fuck dare he keep making decisions for me? Couldn't he see that I was bleeding inside and that I needed the pain to help me bring some sort of sanity into my life before the pain inside me would rip me apart? And how dare he use his size advantage against me, and press his body against mine when his proximity wasn't welcome?

"Let me down, Jett," I repeated, this time squeezing more icy determination into my voice.

"I won't. Not until you calm yourself," he said in my ear, nuzzling my neck. The skin where his lips touched me prickled when he inhaled deeply. "You look cute when you're angry, you know that? If you keep being like this, I'll be forced to keep you close to me the whole day."

"It's not funny."

"No, to you, it isn't." He laughed in my ear, and my

heart melted a few more inches. God, how much I wanted to strangle him in that instant.

"I hate you," I said, furious at him. But I hated myself even more for not seeing it coming. Hated the way my heart raced just because I was nestled in his arms. Hated that I had the unwilling wish for him to kiss me, touch me and hold me when I had to focus on being angry.

"No, you don't, Brooke," Jett said matter-of-factly. "That's just an excuse for how much you love me."

God. He was so right. I was that weak. A wave of hopelessness and despair rattled me. Even when he made fun of me, I still melted when he laughed. Tears welled in my eyes.

"No, I really hate you. Like *hate* hate you," I lied. "I hate your guts. I hate that I loved you once. I hate that you are…like this." My voice and body were shaking, which was bad enough. But it was worse that my heart made somersaults, ready to give in to the annoying weakness I felt for him.

"Like what? Saving you from yourself?" He chuckled. "I would say I'm quite noble."

I scoffed, marveling at the size of his ego. "You're no gentleman, Jett."

"And you're not exactly sweet honey."

"Fuck you." I kicked under me, but my feet only hit the air.

"I would love to," he whispered. "I want you to want me. To fuck you until you can't walk straight.'

His words aroused me, his touch fueled the fire within me, but more than that he infuriated me to the core.

"I really hope that someday karma slaps you in the face before I do," I said through gritted teeth.

He laughed and my heart fluttered. "Hate is a good thing Brooke, you know? At least you're talking. It's so much better than you shutting me out."

"I'm shutting you out?" I tried to turn around with no success. Instead, I was forced to endure his lips grazing my earlobes. "Have you lost your mind? You're the one who's keeping secrets."

"For which I had a reason."

"The fuck you did." I tried to move, but it was impossible. "Let me go, Jett."

"I promise once you calm yourself, I'll let go of you."

"If you don't let me go now, I swear I'll—" I took a sharp breath, considering my words.

"What? You'll hate the way I kiss you?"

I should have seen it coming, and yet it still took me by surprise. His teeth grazed my neck softly a moment before his lips brushed my skin.

"You…"

My words were cut short by the door being thrown open and Brian walking in. Both Jett and I turned to regard him.

"What the fuck, dudes! I can hear your screaming all the way upstairs," he shouted. "What the fuck's going on?"

"Stay out of it, Brian." Jett's voice came calm and composed, but he didn't let go of me.

"Hey, bro. This is my place, so show some fucking respect. Some people have to sleep," Brian shouted before his voice dropped a notch.

"Brooke?" Brian looked at me. Even from the distance, I could see the sudden hint of an amused grin as his gaze brushed over our strange embrace. "Is Jett bothering you?"

"Yeah, as a matter of fact he is." I stared at him in the hope he'd jump in and get Jett put some much-needed distance between us.

But Brian made no such move.

I pointed behind him in case he missed that Jett was standing a bit too close for comfort.

"Big time. He's quite annoying," I added, expecting him to get the hint.

"That he is," he confirmed. "But I'm glad you have it all under control."

What?

What?

"We're just having a little discussion, " Jett chimed in. "Right, Brooke?"

I tried to turn to regard him, ready to do whatever it

took to get him to loosen his tight grip on me, but before I knew it, he let go. I straightened my skirt, my breath coming hard and heavy. My hair and face felt like a hot mess, and I was sure I looked like we just had fun in a haystack rather than a heated discussion.

Inside I was raging. My legs were trembling. My heart was pounding. And my pulse was racing. The moment Brian would leave the room, I promised myself to kick Jett really hard if he ever pulled that stunt again.

"All right." Brian nodded, unconvinced. "If you can't keep from shouting and stomping like a herd of elephants to a minimum level, I will throw you both into building two. Is that understood?"

"Loud and clear," Jett said behind me, amused. "There won't be any problems, boss. No need to lock us up in building two. We'll do as you please. Of course, your well-being is our priority number one."

I snorted loudly, both at Jett's sarcasm and Brian's warning. Maybe building two was the most poorly furnished place—that part was true—but it was still amazing with a huge indoor cinema and a beautiful spiral staircase and plenty of room for everything. I was hardly any sort of punishment. In fact, I would have moved in anytime.

"Brooke?" Brian asked.

"Sure. There won't be any problems." I nodded in agreement.

"You better keep it that way," Brian barked. "I've had enough drama this week. I don't need more of it."

Brian gave us another cautionary look and then he turned around and walked out. For a second I considered hurrying after him, if only to escape the clutches of my weak heart and the conversation I suddenly no longer wanted to have.

Too late.

The door closed and we were back to being alone, back to where we had started. I stared at the closed door, not daring to turn out of fear of plunging into new depths of despair at the entire situation. Come to think of it, I would have loved to hear some of Brian's drama. Any distraction would have been better than dealing with my own life.

All the energy I had saved for this fight was gone, dissipating the moment I realized that if Jett wanted to leave there was nothing I could do to change his mind. He was a free man.

"Brooke?" His voice had become soft, tender and my skin started to prickle as he stepped behind me again.

I shook my head in sadness. "Don't."

His hand touched my shoulder. My knees weakened as he turned me around. There was no smile on his lips. Just sadness. He reminded me of an old lonely tree, the leaves scattering in a thousand directions. The withering of a rose. The cold winter brushing away the last leaf. Just sadness and the promise of winter coming, announcing that everything colorful, everything pretty, would fade away—in time.

"You promised you'd never leave me," I whispered. My voice shook and a new set of tears began to trickle down my cheeks.

"I have to," he whispered. "I explained my reasons, but you chose not to believe me. What does that say about you? You don't trust me and I feel you never will."

"You're wrong about that." I tore myself out of his grip. Feeling the meaning of his words, hearing them—it all felt so true, as if the lies I had told myself was a mere blindfold, and his words had the power to remove it.

He was right, and yet I still didn't want to admit it.

"You could still stay, Jett," I whispered.

For me. For our baby.

"Well, I don't think it's a good idea to stay. What choice do I have but to go away?"

"There's always a choice, Jett. You said so yourself back in Italy."

"Trust me, in this one situation there isn't." He looked at me hard. His stance was rigid, and his jaw clenched, and for the first time I wondered if he was trying to run away from the law, like I had tried to run away from him in fear of getting hurt.

Still, I had to hear it from him. If I didn't get an answer

from him, I'd always feel like the truth had eluded me.

"Why?" I asked and the room grew silent again.

"Have you forgotten that I am busy trying to kill you?" Jett said eventually, "So I can finally get my hands on your old grand estate that I so desperately seek? That's a real life inspiration, you know? Siding with my brother. Raping others and killing them…now that's fun." His voice was dripping with bitterness and sarcasm. His eyes shimmered with a dangerous glint, and there was just the hint of a sad smile on his lips. Suddenly I knew he wasn't just being sarcastic; he was genuinely shocked by my assumptions about him and now he was telling me what he thought I wanted to hear. I couldn't blame him. I had accused him of all of those things and more during our last fight.

"Is that one of the reasons why you're moving to Chicago?" I asked breathlessly.

"No. It's the *only* reason, Brooke." His eyes searched mine. "You made it clear enough that you want me out of your life and that's exactly what I'm giving you," he said. "I can't stay with someone who believes I'm capable of killing a human being for money or power. I love you, Brooke. I really do, but there is no point in staying if you think I'm capable of hurting you. I'd rather kill myself than see you hurt. I'd rather go away than make you feel unsafe around me."

"I didn't really believe that when I said it," I whispered.

189

Somehow it didn't come out right. It sounded as though I was lying to myself. I probably was.

At the images of me Googling him, and sneaking around his apartment in a desperate search of proof, I felt shame pouring through me at the way I assumed the worst about him and yet hoped for the best. From the look of it, Jett sensed my earlier doubts about him.

His disappointment in me was so apparent, my heart lurched.

"I'm not so sure about that," he whispered. "You took it into account that I would harm you, and that's all that matters. You showed me how little trust you had in me. Can you guess how thinking so little of me made me feel?"

His tone sounded hurt, angry and spiteful. He was hurt and I couldn't blame him, but how could I explain to his stubborn self that there were reasons why I did everything that I did? That a set of events, not necessarily created by him, smudged my trust in him.

"Can you guess how seeing you kiss Tiffany made me feel?" I retorted.

His eyes narrowed on me and the glint of anger increased just a little. I had never seen his eyes ablaze with so much anger—their green color so green it could have poisoned or conquered a soul. Right now he was conquering me with the depth he was regarding me.

Towering over me, his large size intimidating me, my

pulse started to race. As Jett regarded me, his irises darkened, matching his mood that I knew was plummeting to new depths. He stepped toward me—so close I could feel his breath on me.

"Let's just be honest, Brooke," he whispered. "Compared to you, I can control myself. Just because Tiffany and I share a history, I would never have fucked her again. Never. And that applies to all other women out there. And do you know why? I didn't need my needs fulfilled, because I already had everything with you. But you?" He gave me an accusatory glare that made me flinch. "You couldn't control yourself when you thought I was Check."

Ouch.

Talk about bitchiness.

I gaped at him in shock.

In the silence, he grabbed his gloves that were lying on the floor next to his bottle of water and walked over to the training mats and the rest of the equipment. His face resembled a mask of ice as he pulled on the gloves, then started lifting free weights, his biceps straining from the effort.

"How dare you!" I said through clenched teeth, feeling anger pouring back into me. "You make it sound like I really slept with another guy."

"Correct me if I'm wrong, but you could have," he muttered, continuing to lift the weights. They looked like they weighed a ton, and yet Jett made it look it was barely a fly.

I opened my mouth, then closed it again.

Fuck, he was right.

My drink had been spiked and it really could have been anyone I brought home. But he still had no right to say that. He had no right to be angry when he was the one who started all the problems. It dawned on me that it was going to be a long day. It might even become our biggest fight yet.

Chapter 19

"FUCK YOU." I crossed my arms over my chest as I stared Jett down. "Maybe that's exactly what I wanted to happen."

He stopped in midair, his eyes narrowing at my words, and his face changed into a mask of anger.

"Say that again?"

There was just a hint of danger in his voice, the kind of tone that matched his black tribal tattoo—the one symbolizing power and dominance. The kind of tone that brought a smile to my lips.

Holy mother of pearls.

He was angry. No, make that fuming. He was like a wild lion, ready to pounce on me and swallow me whole.

I raised my chin defiantly and shrugged.

"Fuck you?" I suggested, innocently.

He put the weights down and turned to face me fully with a glower that made my panties wet.

"No, the other stuff that you just said. About what you want," he prodded. "Say that again."

I bit my lip at how marvelously sexy he sounded when he was pissed—as if his aura was nothing but the form and power of a nuclear bomb, able to tear off my clothes and burn me. And I wanted to be burned all right, all the way to my core.

"You heard me the first time," I said with just a hint of a smile. "If there were another guy, I would have done him." I let the words roll slowly over my tongue. "*Real good.*"

He cocked his head, his eyes fixed on me. Even from where I stood I could see the waves of jealousy and fury wafting over. It pleased me that I had that effect on him. That he wasn't so immune to emotions either. That he was as jealous as me. I liked the idea of having the upper hand for a change and being able to pierce through his sturdy armor. That was my last thought before his steps echoed closer, each one of them slow and measured.

In the silence around us I noticed just how quiet he had become. How my skin reacted to his presence and how my heart hammered against my chest so hard that I was sure everyone in the building would hear it. Finally, his hand touched my hair. With a determined pull, he removed the clip and my hair fell down in a cascade of ringlets. He tangled his hand in them and pulled me close until his hot breath was on my lips.

"Just to make one thing clear, you'll never fuck another guy," Jett whispered low enough for me to hear it, enough to send a tremble down my spine.

My brows shot up in mock amusement. "And why wouldn't I do that?"

"Because you're mine, Brooke," he whispered. "And I don't share."

My heart skipped a beat as I peered into his dark green eyes and I shrank back from the intensity. I tried to laugh, but the sound remained trapped in my throat. He sounded so serious it scared me. I wondered what he'd do if I disobeyed.

"Is that why you were at the club?" I asked breathlessly. "To stalk me? To make sure there wouldn't be anyone but you?"

"No, far from it." His voice sounded hoarse as his eyes bore into mine, penetrating the deepest layers around my being.

"Then why would you go there?" I narrowed my eyes on him.

"You know why. The same reason I followed you to Italy." His gaze brushed my face and settled on my lips.

Under his intensive, probing glance, I felt exposed and heat began to radiate through me. Slowly the corners of his lips twitched. He must have known the impact his body had on me, or why else would his cockiness and massive ego begin to resurface?

"Remind me to finish this conversation later when we're done," he whispered.

"Done with what?"

My breath hitched when he pulled me to him, crushing my mouth against his. Beneath his clothes, I could feel he was hard—for me. He pressed his bottom lip between mine, forcing me to open my mouth only to run his tongue over mine in a long heated mind-blowing kiss.

Holy cow.

The guy knew how to kiss, and kiss good.

Talk about marvelously good.

My whole body was on fire, begging him to set me free, urging me to get the closeness I had been missing.

Screw the fight.

I wanted him bad. I wanted him now—when he still had that dangerous glint in his eyes and was looking so dangerously handsome, his half-naked body a sinful temptation.

As his tongue dipped into my mouth, swirling in and out in slow, hard moves, my head began to spin harder and my knees grew weaker. Deep inside of me I could feel something pulsating to life.

Longing. Desire.

I need it, needed him. And from the way his hardness kept pressing against me, he needed it, too—in whatever way. There was no doubt about the fact that I was more than willing to sleep with him.

"Don't mistake my lust for weakness," I whispered.

Or forgiveness, for that matter.

"Don't worry. I won't." His lips curled into the most stunning smile, flashing his perfect teeth, all straight and white.

I sucked in my breath as he pushed my hair to one side, only for his lips to hover over my skin. He was so rough and yet so demanding in his movement, his touch perfect, experienced, determined—leaving me in perfect balance of want and need. His touch, warm and soft, sent shivers down my spine. I moaned ever so slightly. It had been so long. Too long.

The anticipation of touching him, of feeling him inside me was growing bigger by the second. I knew I was about to lose my pathetic self-control. My hands reached for his training shorts, sliding inside the waistband, and then I pulled down. My breath hitched in my throat as his erection jerked out.

He wasn't just big.

He was impressive—like a king among queens. I flicked

my tongue over my lips as my fingers tenderly moved over the slick crown and my hands were about to run down his hard shaft when his fingers closed around mine, holding me captive in my movement.

"You've lost that privilege," he whispered, pulling my wrist behind my back. "From this moment on, I'll be making all the decisions."

"What?" I whispered as his lips crashed on mine again, cutting off my words. I moaned when he circled my tongue, sucking it deep into his mouth like a wild tornado on fire, and he began to unbutton my shirt with one hand, the other holding my wrist. I shuddered at the way his fingers touched my skin whenever a button came loose while his tongue continued to conquer my mouth.

After what seemed like an eternity, he removed my shirt. The coldness of the room hit my bare skin and I sucked in my breath.

And then his hand touched the zip of my skirt. Somewhere inside my brain, I could hear that we were about to embark on public make-up-sex, that anyone could enter the hall and catch us in mid-action, but I didn't care. Jett was the only man who was capable of making me forget the world around me. He was the only person, who was like ecstasy—dangerous and addicting.

Lowering myself onto the hard mat, I pulled him on top of me, breathing in the scent of his aftershave.

Before I knew it, I was naked and Jett accommodated his weight on top of me, his knees on either side of my body, pausing, waiting.

Confused, I looked up, unsure why he was watching me when he grabbed my wrists and leaned into me. I didn't mind. It was an opportunity for me to stare at his wide shoulders and beautiful, tattooed chest.

Holy pearls.

His chest was so broad, his arms so strong they could carry a woman until the end of time.

"Brooke?" he whispered, drawing my attention back from his muscles and the throbbing between my legs. I couldn't help but think how much I loved him calling my name. As if I belonged only to him, as if I was the only woman in his world. The only one that mattered now that I was lying beneath his hard body, my entire being turned to liquid.

"Yeah?"

He smiled gently as he looked at me. "I'm so pissed off at you."

"Me, too." I returned his smile. "I'm raging."

He shook his head and the smile disappeared. "No. You don't understand." I narrowed my eyes as his hands slowly moved away from my wrists and started circling my breasts, focusing on my hardening nipples. "I'm so jealous I don't think I can share you with anyone. Ever."

"Then we have something in common."

"Do we?" He cocked his eyebrow. "Because I doubt it."

My breath hitched in my throat, the words stuck in my throat, as his hands moved up my arms, then alongside my collarbones, one thumb stopping at the sensitive hollow of my neck, the sternal notch. With a soft movement, he tilted my head to one side and then he began to kiss me, sending a tremble through my body as his lips settled on my earlobe.

"Do you have any idea what I'm going to do to you for all the things you said?" he whispered in my ear. His voice was so deep and low, full of dark promises to unmake and punish me.

"No." In spite of my attempt at infusing some much needed confidence into my tone, my voice broke. "But what makes you think I'd let you do that?"

"You want me to, Miss Stewart," he whispered, rising up on his knees and his hand moved between my legs. "I can sense your needs."

His confidence made me not only nervous, I felt like I was having my first time all over again. The hint of a southern accent in his angry tone was even sexier than I could have dreamed of.

If Jett Mayfield weren't the owner of a successful company, he would have made his fortune by becoming a narrator. Or judging from his body, he would have been a model. I smiled at the image of him posing, his muscles glorified by the camera.

And then I remembered that he had no idea that I had tried my hand at posing as a pin-up girl. I had no idea how he'd react if he found out.

"I have many needs," I said, pushing the dark thoughts to the back of my mind. "You don't know half of them."

"Then I'd better make sure to find all of them and fulfill them one by one." He grinned as he dipped one long finger slowly into my wet sex. His eyes locked on me as he spun his finger, pulling it out slowly, the motion making me wetter and hotter before he sucked it into his mouth. "Tasty." He grinned. "Now don't even pretend you don't enjoy this. You're into this…a lot."

Damn. He was good.

Inside, I was wet and ready for him.

I wasn't just into this. I was into *him*.

My head was throbbing. My legs were trembling. And my heart was racing at the way he kept looking at me with that dangerous glint in his eyes. As his thumb kept rubbing my clit, my pulse spiked and heat rushed to my cheeks.

"I'm more than just into this, Jett," I whispered, thinking of the crime scene evidence I had hidden in the car. Of all the things I had done for him, without having any answers. His face flickered with amusement. I wasn't sure he heard me or the seriousness in my tone.

Jett leaned forward and kissed me deeply, so tender that there was no way to say whose air I breathed. Was it mine or his? Was it air intermingled? Or was my passion the product of us two?

It struck me that I wanted him to leave his mark on me, something I could always treasure. If his kiss could have burned me then I would have wanted him to kiss me harder. More fiercely, until the feeling lasted for all eternity.

His hands caressed my shoulders, moving lower and between my legs again, brushing them apart. I closed my eyes, savoring his touch, his breath on my face, the warmth of his body.

I should have seen it coming, but it still took me by surprise when he entered me. It was slow and tender as he pushed inside my core, into my being. His gaze looked at me with a depth that equaled the way he penetrated me—demanding, possessive—just the way I needed it. Maybe it was the gentleness of a usually primitive act, or that there was nothing dirty in it, but it felt right, like two beings trapped in a cocoon. With the heat flooding over my body, I let out a deep moan, and lifted my hips against his in need for more, closing my eyes to enjoy the moment.

"Look at me," Jett whispered. His voice sounded hoarse and I opened my eyes, my breath coming heavy. My heart skipped a beat as I peered into his green eyes and noticed that his mouth had softened as his thick shaft moved inside me, stretching me, filling every last corner. And yet something felt different.

"Do you love me?" he asked at last.

I drew a long breath. Here I was, in the middle of an argument, lying on the mat, with him moving inside me, and he was asking if I loved him.

I swallowed hard. How was I supposed to answer that? With my body so exposed and open for him I was barely able to think straight as every slow thrust sent a new wave of pleasure through me, announcing my imminent release. My hands grabbed his shoulders, my fingers dug into his skin. That was the only answer I could give him.

Anytime now the thrusts would send me over the edge. As though sensing my impending orgasm, Jett replaced his slow thrust with even slower moves—painfully slow moves that sent the whole room spinning and my insides clenching for more. My breath was barely more than a shudder. I could feel every rub, every motion, every drop of moisture of him inside me. He pulled out, only to push in deeper, his thrust hitting my core. His eyes never left mine as he continued to slowly thrust inside me, his body moving against me. I moaned, shifting my hips to let him slide in just a little bit deeper. Hot waves of fire shook my abdomen as he impaled my flesh and I lifted my hips to give him deeper access when he suddenly pulled out again, only to let the slick head of his erection nudge my entrance.

Ever so slowly he plunged in and stopped until I could feel nothing but him pulsating inside me, waiting...waiting for what?

Right. For my answer.

"What kind of stupid question is that?" I asked.

"Just be honest."

"It's not like you are."

"Well, I try to be." He moistened his lips. His beautiful kissable seductive lips. I swallowed, both intimidated by the question and the rising need inside me. "If I love you?"

He nodded. "Yeah."

His intent gaze landed on me again and for a few seconds there was silence between us. At last, he stirred again,

"Do you, Brooke?" he probed. "Do you love me?"

I looked up. His eyes peered intently at me, waiting, watching. Doubting. It felt as though the question was different. It felt anxious. Careful. Uncertain. Almost as if he had started to believe my lies at some point.

All those years I had the unprecedented and unspoken belief that even the most sparkling stone of a relationship would become dull. Not so with Jett. He was a multi-faceted diamond that blinded me with its brilliance and hardness. And right now, he was cutting me into the core, his eyes resting on me, and his hardness teasing me mercilessly by staying lodged deep inside me without moving. I quivered beneath him, my body pleading for more.

"I do," I whispered. "Sadly. Maybe even too much."

"Then tell me you're mine."

"You're killing me," I whispered, feeling like I was about to cry from sheer pleasure. "Can't it wait until later?"

He grinned. "That's just the start of the punishment I'm about to give you." Wedging himself between my knees and lifting my legs a little higher, he forced his shaft deeper inside me, filling every inch so slowly I felt like helping myself to get the release I so desperately craved.

Damn.

I should have seen it coming. He was going to make me beg and plead. He was going to torture by filling me, impaling me, building up my orgasm without letting me come. A stroke of passion rushed up my spine like lightening.

Damn him.

I was so damn near and yet he stalled.

He carried a weapon more dangerous than a gun. And right now this weapon stretched me, giving me the feeling of being invaded. Now I understood what *La petite m*ort meant. If Jett kept going like this, I would experience the little death and it wouldn't be pretty.

"Jett, please. Don't make me plead."

His lips twitched. "You'll have to do better than that."

His erection plunged another inch into me, building a bigger, growing momentum until I felt I might just be about to pass out.

"Say you're mine, Brooke." His hands grabbed my wrists and pulled them above my head until I could do nothing but look at him. His breath brushed my mouth, stealing my air, my oxygen, my soul. There was no him and me, only two hearts.

"I'm yours," I moaned. Pleased with my answer, he started to move. Slow, deliberate, painful moves.

"You forgot to call my name." He laughed hoarsely.

It was in that moment that our eyes connected with a depth that made me tremble like music did to my soul. As he kept moving inside me, dissolving my sensitive flesh, his breath on my face, there was nothing but him and the hardness of his spear penetrating me. He kissed me with a passion as if his lips had always belonged on mine. Or maybe it was I who had always belonged to him.

"Mine," he whispered. "You'll always be mine, Brooke. As I will be yours. And that's my promise."

His tongue sucked mine deep into his mouth and he slammed harder into me until our bodies began to tremble, ripe with orgasm. I closed my eyes and let myself melt into him, savoring the sensation in the knowledge that everything was right.

Everything was okay. I was safe.

I could feel it.

With my heart pounding against my chest I could feel myself falling into one special place—where passion and tension collided to create a color so beautiful it took my breath away. Jett shuddered, his hot moisture spilling deep inside me as an orgasm rippled through him, pouring his essence into me, and then I came.

Chapter 20

WE WERE LYING on the floor, side by side—on our backs, staring up at the ceiling. The passion was gone, leaving us in the darkness of something ominous that threatened to destroy the sanctuary we had built through lovemaking. Seconds passed, which turned into minutes with us both afraid to speak first. It was then that I realized if I wanted answers, I had to be careful with Jett. If neither of us took the plunge, then there would always be a misunderstanding and poison would eventually seep into our relationship, staining it, damaging it beyond repair. I didn't want to go back to that cold, dark place of insecurities, a world filled with secrets and words unspoken. Conversely, if we began to communicate there was always the small possibility of another fight, and I wasn't sure I was ready for that.

So what will it be, Stewart? Fight or silence? Anger or resentment?

One wrong word, one wrong action, and it all might just go down the drain. Sex brought us together, but any sort of tension could easily tear us apart. From what I understood, Jett's issue was his fear that I might be dating other men, which were fears very similar to mine, except my problem with him was a lot bigger. A lot more dangerous. Deciding to speak out, I swallowed the lump in my throat.

"Back at the hotel, I felt like you went behind my back when you visited Nate. And then, at the bar, seeing you with another woman, broke me," I started, not daring to look at him. "I wanted to get back at you. Hurt you as much as you hurt me in the hope that another guy would help me make this even. That's why I went out that night." My gaze scanned his face for clues to what he was thinking. He continued to look at the ceiling, his arms crossed under his head, but his breathing had become quiet. "But even with Check, I still kept seeing you. When I closed my eyes that night, I still wished it was you who was making love to me. And it was still you, who turned me on in my thoughts."

Silence ensued for a moment and then Jett turned to face me. He glanced at me with a depth that made my skin tremble. "So does it mean you're not over me?" he asked quietly. A soft smile lit up his gorgeous lips and I almost choked on my emotions.

"I'm not over you," I whispered. "And I'd be lying if I said that I wanted things to be over. But—" I paused, struggling for words, as the images of Gina's face popped into my mind. "I just feel that your secrets are destroying our relationship. I can't deal with them anymore. I'm so sick of us not knowing what's going on in the other's life."

He propped up on one elbow and inched closer until I could almost feel his breath on my skin. And suddenly his lips curled upward in a sexy smile. After all the drama and the fighting, being in his arms again seemed unreal and unrealistic, and his smile wasn't the reaction I expected.

I frowned at him, unsure if he was making fun of me.

"What's so funny?" I asked, confused.

"What you just said. Sounds like Check wasn't successful in making you forget me. Yesterday you claimed we were over. Today you want to make this relationship work. That tells me you want to be with me. *Truly* be with me."

"Well, I never wanted it to end," I admitted, regarding him. When he continued smiling at me, I brushed my hair out of my eyes, considering my words. "Jett, our relationship's not what bothers me. It's all the secrets you're keeping that destroy us. I feel like I can never trust you fully

210

if you keep things hidden from me."

He looked at me blankly. His smile disappeared, and I felt a hint of disappointment at the fact that he was bottling up again.

I wanted for him to open up to me, not to ignore me, to spill whatever he was hiding in his mind. Good or bad. It didn't even matter. Bad wasn't even that bad. I could get accustomed to it. I would have tried to understand what I otherwise couldn't.

"Don't you have *anything* to tell me?" I prompted when he didn't reply.

"I told you already. I have my reasons, Brooke." His voice was still quiet, but there was a hint of authority behind it that didn't allow room for questioning.

I wet my lips nervously, considering my words carefully. When they came out, they sounded vulnerable and shaky. "Why is it so hard for you to tell me? You can trust me. You know that, don't you?"

"I do, but I can't tell you. It's not possible."

"Why not?"

"Because it's not that simple." He let out a deep breath. "I know you have questions." He paused and took a deep breath. "But like I said, it's complicated. I'm not sure you'd understand and I'm not willing to risk it."

My shoulders dropped. After everything, we were back to square one. He still wouldn't confide in me. Or wanted

211

to. I was far from getting the answers I needed. The knowledge that he was leaving me in the dark again was tearing me apart.

"It's more complicated than being a primary murder suspect, you mean?" The words left my mouth before I could stop them.

He grimaced. "A murder...*what*?" Every muscle in his face tensed, but his lips belied his shock.

"I was there," I said matter-of-factly.

"Where?"

"In your apartment."

There was a stunned silence. I couldn't believe I had blurted that out in desperation. He stared at me. I could see his surprise, his thoughts processing my words.

"I saw her things," I whispered. "It bothers me that you didn't tell me that the police is looking for evidence to find Gina's killer. Why all this secrecy and—"

"Hold on," he cut me short, his eyes narrowing me. "Just hold on. What are you talking about?"

"You don't know what I'm talking about?" My voice came out louder than intended. "The girl you talked to in the coffee shop and was killed later that day."

He continued to stare at me. I could almost hear his nervousness, which turned me instantly anxious.

"What girl, Brooke?"

I looked at him in sheer disbelief, my voice failing me.

Stay calm, Stewart. Play it cool. He might be playing clueless, but you know better than to trust blindly.

I took a deep breath and let it out slowly. "The detective said he took you in for questioning, Jett. There's no reason for you to pretend that you don't know what I'm talking about."

"I *don't* know what you're talking about." His voice dropped to an icy whisper. "What detective?"

Oh, God.

He was good.

I pressed my mouth into a tight line. Now that my thoughts had become my nightmares and my fears my pursuers, he just couldn't see how important his honesty was.

"How can you still lie to me?" My voice was barely more than a croak. "I saw the pictures, Jett. Don't you get it?" I got up and furiously buttoned up my dress. Eventually I grabbed my bag and coat from where I had left them on the floor, ready to walk out. "I'm going. There's no point in me staying if you can't even admit the truth." From the periphery of my eyes, I watched Jett get up, pull up his slacks, and then head for me. He reached me in two long strides, his height both intimidating and arousing me.

"Brooke, please!" He grabbed my arm, but his grip was tender, begging me to listen rather than gluing me to the spot. "I swear I'm telling you the truth. I have no clue."

"You have no clue?" I turned to him, my face ablaze. "What about your brother? Will you pretend you don't know about him either?"

"I can explain that." He sighed and wiped his palm over his face. "You'll see there's a perfect explanation."

I yanked my arm away. "I don't want to hear your perfect explanations about Nate. I want the truth about everything, which you so obviously can't give."

He touched my arm again.

"*Please.*" He never said please like that. "Let's talk about this. Give me a chance to explain about Nate."

"You'll answer all of my questions?" I asked doubtfully, my gaze scanning his face for any signs that he was bluffing.

"If you listen and stay, then yes, I will."

I drew a sharp breath and let it out slowly. Crossing my arms over my chest, I stared him down. "Okay. You have one minute. Spill."

"That's all I need." He wet his lips, taking his time to reply. "Do you remember when I said that the ETNAD club has many powerful and famous people involved and they are fanatic to keep their identities protected? That in order to hide their identity from the outside world they go to great length by hiring the best lawyers and worse?"

"Yeah, but what's that to do with you?"

He held up his hand, silencing me. "Just listen." When I nodded, he continued, "The only reason I visited Nate in prison is because they need him for a set-up. The evidence the police impounded is not enough to get each and every member behind bars. Some of them are high-ranked politicians and, and with their reputations at stake, let's say they're more than happy to pay for certain privileges, like making evidence disappear. So, my brother agreed to work with police to expose the remaining members of his elite club in exchange for having his sentence reduced." Jett paused, letting the words sink in. "In the eyes of the public, including the elite members, he's a free man, but he's not. Nate's simply cooperating with the police."

I stared at him, feeling an ice-cold knot twisting inside my stomach.

"Oh, God," I murmured at last. "What if he runs away?"

And kills me, I wanted to add but didn't.

"Brooke, they are keeping him on surveillance. It won't happen."

"You mean he's wearing wires and an ankle monitor and all?"

Jett nodded.

I eyed him wearily. "He's cooperating?"

He nodded again. "Trust me, Brooke. I don't like it either. But I don't have a say in the matter. The only reason I visited him was because I wanted to know what he's doing, where he's going, who he's talking to. I had to make sure he stays the hell away from you."

"How long will he be out for?"

"I don't know. Two weeks, one month, I guess," Jett said.

I swallowed the thick lump in my throat.

Jett's brother had been involved in an illegal elite club that kidnapped, raped and killed for fun. It was the same club that had kidnapped me when Nate wanted to kill me to get his hands on the Italian estate I had inherited. Having his sentence reduced wasn't what I had hoped for.

"How long have you known?" I asked.

Jett looked down, evading my questioning gaze. "Longer than I wanted," he whispered. "Like I said, sadly, there was not enough evidence to tie them all down, which is where Nate's supposed to come in."

"And you trust that he'll do as requested of him?"

He cocked his head to the side. "I know my brother. He'll want the shortest sentence, even if that means betraying his friends. It doesn't, however, mean that he's a changed man."

My heart slammed against my chest. "If you've known for a long time, why didn't you tell me sooner?"

His jaw set and he hesitated, probably considering his words. "I didn't want you to get involved."

"Involved in what?"

"Nate and all the shit that surrounds him," Jett said. I

could understand that, but still.

I narrowed my eyes. "Jett, you could have told me. You know that, don't you?"

"It was a mistake that I didn't. I know it now." He smiled gently. "I did something stupid, and I'm sorry. Now you know the truth why I kept this from you."

I didn't return his smile, unconvinced by his words. Instead, I kept looking at him, challenging him, waiting for him to spill the beans but he stayed as tightlipped as before.

"What about the other secrets, Jett?" I asked. "Do you have anything else to tell? Anything at all?"

He froze, his grimace signaling that he might just be about to blast me off. "Yeah, that's the thing, what other things, Brooke?"

"What about the girl they said you killed? Or about your car showing traces of you running her over. Or that you're a murder suspect. Or what about the letter you left me at four in the morning, scaring the hell out of me?" I asked in desperation, feeling like I was going mad.

He stepped back, eyeing me hard. "Jesus. Where did you get those ideas?" He stared at me furiously. "Tell me who the fuck tells you those lies and I will beat this motherfucker up."

I shrank back by the intensity of his words, but then composed myself just as quickly. "It was a detective I met at work." Seeing Jett's confused glance, I remembered that

Jett didn't know about the job, and added, "It's a long story. I got a new job, by the way. Me and two girls I met there went out the same night you picked me up to celebrate my job offer. Anyway, one of the girls was killed, and the detective questioned all of us. He told me about you."

God, it all sounded so crazy. Even though it had barely been a few days, my life was slowly beginning to sound more complicated than a soap opera. Maybe I should start recording my everyday occurrences to keep track. I almost expected Jett to start inquiring about the new job when he shook his head in confusion, keeping silent, processing. He looked at me as if I had told him I just had brunch with the devil.

"Her name was Gina. Maybe you knew her?" I added, hoping the new bit of information would jolt his memory. He didn't say anything. I waited impatiently, unsure what to make of his silence.

"Do you know how you sound?" He said at last. The glint in his eyes matched the thick waves of tension wafting from him. I took a step back and surveyed him.

"Trust me, I know perfectly how I sound. Like someone who lost a screw, right?"

He stared me down. "That's about right, Brooke."

"But do *you* know in what kind of situation you are, Jett?" I asked. "Apparently, you killed two people." I held out my hand. "Not my words. The detective's. He said you bought immunity, and told me that you had your car reported stolen. He told me that your car was found with plenty of traces."

"A detective, huh?" He looked at me as though I had just gone completely crazy. As if I was the one who made up the lies. I remained quiet, watching his reaction, not avoiding his furious glances. "Was Tina one of the girls you were with the night I picked you up at the club?" he asked quietly.

"Gina," I corrected, narrowing my eyes. "Yeah, she was. How do you know?"

Please tell me you know her. Tell me something. Anything at all. Please.

"It was just a wild guess considering you said a girl died that night and you seem to have known her."

My shoulders slumped, disappointment and defeat washing over me. Suddenly, the situation wasn't just scary, it was overwhelming—a burden on my shoulders, threatening to nail me down, making sure I would never get up. I had come in hope for answers only to find that the whole conversation with Jett—except for Nate—was going nowhere. As though I was stuck in a crazy labyrinth, I had no idea which way to go, what to do, not even sure if there was any sort of escape from the fear that had been following me around all day.

I didn't just feel helpless, I felt like there was nothing

more I could do. What was worse, I felt like Jett didn't understand me; as though he'd never share that burden with me, and that I was all alone. For once I wished life weren't so complicated. If he had just told me what was going on, if he only tried to explain, maybe I would have been able to understand him and start solving what needed to be cleared. But the fact that he kept pretending to have no clue meant that he'd stifle that trepidation inside me, which only managed to make me even more wary of him and the other secrets he might be keeping.

"I don't know if I can trust you, Jett." I almost choked on my voice and cleared my throat. "You can't even admit that you left me a letter last night?" A tear ran down my cheek. I brushed my hand over my face, hiding from him if only for a moment—my vulnerability so naked I was sure that any cruel word could blast a hole in my skin. "I came here looking for answers and you make everything worse by denying any knowledge. Why can't you just once tell me the truth and help me understand what's going on? Why can't you just tell me the secrets you keep from me and stop…this madness?"

His soft touch stroked my face and his hand cupped my chin, his thumb wiping away the tears, forcing me to look at him.

"I am not accused of murder, Brooke," he said slowly. His voice was calm, but underneath I could hear slight outrage. "My car was not stolen. I didn't send you any letter. I have *absolutely* no clue what you're talking about. I don't even know a detective. The closest I came to any sort of trouble with the law was through my lawyers. I was never questioned for anything."

I swallowed.

"So your car wasn't reported stolen?" I asked incredulously.

"No."

"You were not accused of murderer?"

"Nope," he said slowly.

I stared at him in disbelief.

"What, Brooke? You think I'm some lying sociopath?"

I raised my brows at him. "Are you?"

"Jesus, Brooke. Of course, I'm not." His voice came so low I winced. It made me almost feel bad. If only I had concrete proof that he *wasn't*.

Looking at him, I realized there was no way he could be such a good actor. He looked as shocked as when his father was hurt or when I announced that I was pregnant. Jett wasn't an open book like me, but today I could see the emotions on his usually unreadable face. And right now I could see one thick vein throbbing on his forehead, and his shoulders were all tense, as if he was ready to punch something.

"I don't understand," I whispered. "If you did none of

those things, how come the detective thinks it was you and they found traces of one of the victims on *your* car?"

"Are you sure he's not confusing me with someone else?"

The possibility had crossed my mind, but the police hardly ever made mistakes. Or did they? I turned to him, taking in his worried face. "Pretty sure. I saw pictures of you, Jett. And the detective knew your name." Another shiver ran down my spine as I remembered the details of Gina's gruesome death.

"And he said my car was reported stolen?" he asked incredulously.

I nodded. "And that it had traces of the dead girl's DNA."

Without another word, he grabbed my hand, pulling me along. In less than a minute, we reached the basement where the cars were parked. Jett swung the door open and switched on the lights.

I recognized his car immediately. It was parked in its usual spot, all sparkling and shiny and very expensive, beckoning to me.

"So, do you believe me now?" he whispered. I shook my head, not because I didn't believe him, but because what I was seeing didn't make sense.

"Tell me, Brooke, did this detective show you his badge?" he asked, not waiting for an answer.

"No, he didn't."

He let out a sharp breath and shook his head.

"*What?*" I asked slowly.

He took his time answering. "I think someone's playing a game with you, Brooke. Someone's trying to mess with your head. I don't know what his intention is, if it is to separate us, but I'm sure of one thing," Jett continued, whispering so low my skin began to prickle. "The detective isn't a detective and I want you to stay away from him. Do you hear me?"

Words failed me. I always assumed there was an explanation for everything, but never this possibility. Once more sickness washed over me, and I closed my eyes, feeling suddenly faint. When I opened my eyes again, his forehead was creased with worry.

"Come here." He pulled me to his chest, and I let him. "I love you and that should count for something," he whispered. All the anger was gone, leaving behind worry and gentleness. "I know you don't trust me and I'm fine with that. But make no mistake, I'd never hurt you. I would never kill an innocent. You're safe with me and that's all that matters."

"How can I be sure of that?" My chin trembled. "You say I know you and that you love me, but there are still so many questions unanswered, Jett. You didn't even tell me that you were involved with Tiffany."

He blinked once. Twice.

"You're right, and I'm sorry about that," he whispered, his voice dropping so low I had to strain to understand him, his eyes misting over. "I didn't tell you about Tiffany, because I thought it didn't matter. She was one of many I had."

I looked up. "That's not exactly helpful in figuring you out."

"That might be true, but it doesn't change the fact that I love you. Or that we're expecting a child, and I'd do anything for you."

The room was so quiet his heartbeat sounded like soft rain in my ears. Come to think of it, as I strained harder to listen, I realized it was the splatter of rain splashing against the windows and the roof. It had started raining again. Loud thunder echoed in the distance and I couldn't help but inhale Jett's soothing scent as I recalled the poem about the rain and the tears. Yet I didn't move. In his embrace, I felt like home. It was only when I remembered the things in my car that I stirred.

"Jett?" I murmured, my heart suddenly picking up in speed. "Did you remove my things from your apartment?"

His smile instantly varnished. "No, I wasn't there since Friday, right before we left for the hotel. Why are you asking?"

I hugged my body, then looked up at him. Swallowing

the thick lump in my throat, I took my time with an answer. "There's something I have to tell you, Jett," I whispered. "The girl who was killed, Gina, I found her things at your place. Before I left, I saw two cops talking with the concierge. I think they were there for you."

He stared at me for a full minute, his lips tight, his brows furrowed.

"Are you sure they were there for me?" There was no hint of surprise in his voice. His tone sounded more like he had accepted what I had just told him.

"I'm not certain, but it doesn't change the fact that my things are gone, replaced with hers," I whispered. "Do you understand? Those are the dead girl's belongings. I packed up everything and stashed it all in my car before the cops arrived."

"So, where's everything now?"

"Outside. In my car." My voice broke. "Jett, you're in trouble. The photos showed a body. If what you say is true, that he isn't a detective, I think we have a huge problem. Someone's trying to frame you. And frame you good."

He drew a long breath. "Why did you take her things?"

"I don't know. I—" My voice broke again. Why did I indeed? "I didn't want you to get into trouble, I guess. If the police found her stuff at your place, it would have been impounded as evidence."

"I'm glad you did," he said matter-of-factly.

I watched him grab his towel before leaning in to give me a short kiss on the mouth.

"Where are you going?" I asked, confused.

"I have a feeling it's going to be a long story, so I'm getting us lunch while you go and take a shower. And then you'll tell me everything from the beginning."

"Can I come with you?" I asked.

"I'd rather you stay here if you don't mind." He turned to me with the slightest hint of a smile. "I'll make it quick, babe. Do you want pistachio ice cream as desert?"

I returned his smile. Ever since finding out that I was pregnant, I had been craving for ice cream every day. The fact he remembered it together with so many other little things, made my heart flutter. My stomach growled, reminding me that I hadn't had dinner or breakfast or much of anything, really.

"That'd be great. Thanks. I'm starving," I said. "What about Brian and his rules?"

"Brian?" Jett raised his eyebrows. "I don't give a shit about rules, but I do care about you. Deeply. And right now it's my priority to fulfill my pregnant girlfriend's every wish."

His words made me blush.

In the silence of the room I continued to watch him, my gaze brushing over his sexy back that was now turned to me. Before he opened the door, he hesitated and something heavy settled in the air between us.

"Brooke, earlier when I asked if you loved me, you said you loved me too much, but..." Jett paused. "There is no right way to love. Only one way to love and it is to love fiercely, to love fully and to love passionately. Don't get that wrong. Ever. Same about fighting and trusting me. You need those three things to build a strong relationship."

"How do you know?" I asked.

"How don't you?" His eyes glinted with something else. Amusement. Challenge. Danger.

"Who says I don't?" I whispered, feeling an odd pull of happiness inside my heart as I watched him leave, closing the door behind him. My skin tingled. My whole being trembled. Something rose within me. It was joy, I realized. Joy that he wasn't a killer. That he loved me, wanted me. That Tiffany didn't matter. Joy that my feelings were reciprocated and he cared enough about me—hearing it from him, feeling it with every fiber of my being, sensing the strong waves of worry emanating from him. In that instant I realized that I had never hated him. That, with no exceptions, love didn't need reciprocation to exist. That it didn't matter what he had done, who he had been before meeting me. I would continue to love him unconditionally, no matter what. I had done the right thing.

END OF EPISODE 3

J.C. REED

Jett and Brooke's story continues in the sensual final part in the No Exceptions series,

THE

LOVER'S

PROPOSAL

COMING SPRING 2015

Never miss a release. Use the chance to get a sneak peek, teasers, or win amazing prizes, such as an e-reader of your choice, gift cards, and ARCs by signing up to my newsletter.

As a subscriber, you'll also receive an email reminder on release day:

http://www.jcreedauthor.blogspot.com/p/mailing-list.html

To those, who want to learn more about Brooke's past and the story behind the Lucazzone estate, I welcome you to read the prequel of No Exceptions:

SURRENDER YOUR LOVE
J.C.REED

A THANK YOU LETTER

Thank you for reading any of my books. I hope you enjoyed reading Brooke and Jett's story as much as I enjoyed writing it. If you did, please consider leaving a review as those are hard to come by for indie authors without the huge support of an entire editorial and promotions department.

I also love to hear from my readers. To stay in touch, visit me at the links below. I'm forever grateful and hope you will enjoy my next release.

Jessica C. Reed

Connect with me online:

http://www.jcreedauthor.blogspot.com

http://www.facebook.com/pages/JC-Reed/295864860535849

http://www.twitter.com/jcreedauthor